4/:

RAQUEL + STE[...]

MY LATEST CREATIVE

ENDEAVOR GOTTA LOTS

OF PRACTICAL INFO.

CONGRATULATIONS,

VISIONARY FICTION

THE LIGHTSPACE ULTIMATUM

— EVOLVE OR DIE —

SIDNEY C. WALKER

Published by High Plains Publications
San Diego, California

ISBN: 0962117765
ISBN: 9780962117763

Cover Design: Ken Williams, Jr.; GraphicsQuarter.net.

This book is dedicated to…
the genius and love of your intuitive spirit.

About this book...

Luke thought he was just a guy picking up a beautiful woman in a bar. He had no idea she was about to make him one of the most influential people in the world. Now, his focus, his nerve, and his ability to trust his intuitive instincts will determine whether he becomes a hero for all time or the cause of the end of the human race.

A handful of people have been trained by extraterrestrials on how to reach the euphoric state of mind called *lightspace*. But they were given an ultimatum: *Help Humanity evolve beyond their violent nature, or your species will be destroyed for the good of the Universe.*

This is the story of the LightSpace Project and the people assigned this daunting task. *Can they transform enough people in time to save humans from obliteration?*

Table of Contents

1. Making Contact...

She was perfect. Late twenties, long silky brown hair, bright brown eyes, warm smile, movie star teeth, olive skin, great energy, with a heart-stopping recreational body all decked out in a dark green business suit made from those super-lightweight high-tech fabrics. I couldn't take my eyes off her.

I pretended to look away so it didn't look like I was staring. Years of ice hockey had given me enhanced peripheral vision. If you're going to skate backwards at thirty miles an hour, you learn to see out the back of your head. Still, I hoped no one would notice. Usually the other women in the vicinity picked up on your visual obsession. I hated that. They were wondering why I was staring at her and not at them. I was doing my best to look cool and not get caught drooling.

Breathe, I mumbled to myself. Breathe in, breathe out. Let's see if we can take the energy down a few notches. I'll just watch this beauty for a while. I grabbed the only empty stool around the corner of the bar so my natural line of sight included looking at her. She was talking with two guys, of course. I could tell they were just as excited about her as I was.

1

A smiling Billy Crystal look-alike got my attention from behind the bar and yelled over the crowd noise, "What can I get you?"

"Rusty Nail on the sweet side," I said. I expected him to know what I was talking about. What the heck, I was celebrating the luck of being in the presence of this goddess. I'd have to remember to pace myself after this drink. Too many Rusty Nails had gotten me into trouble. I had officially warned myself.

Time for a strategy meeting. I needed to find a way to start a conversation with Miss Homecoming Queen. I had to find a way to distract her from the two lads she was with. How was I going to do that?

Something I discovered in college that worked well at the nightclubs was to go up to a table of two or more women and say that I was part of a PR team, self-appointed of course. I would say, "I just wanted to make sure you ladies are having a good time." They'd smile and make some kind of nice comment back because they loved the attention and were thrilled that someone cared about whether they were having a good time. Then I'd say, "Are you looking for anyone in particular tonight?" They'd say, "What do you mean?" or "How about the love of my life!" Then I'd say, "Are you looking for a particular kind of guy?"

"Well sure, what have you got?"

I really had their attention then. "Tell me what kind of guy you're looking for. What are your top five qualities?"

If there were three or four women at the table, we were now into a major discussion about what qualities were important, and there was usually some agreement and some disagreement. I'd then point to one of the women and say, "What's your first name?" She'd respond, "Mary Ann." "Okay, Mary Ann, give me your top three qualities."

"Only three? I thought you said I could have five."

"Okay, give me five." I'd say it like that was a major concession. As she started with her qualities, I'd add, "Just a minute," then pull out a little notepad from my vest pocket and write down her name and her top five qualities.

"Athletic, funny, smart, caring, handsome," I repeated back. I would go around the table and write down what the other three wanted. Then I would give my disclaimer. "Now, I can't give you any guarantees, but let me check around and see who's here. As I run into good candidates for you, I will send them over to your table. Be gentle with my guys, give them a chance. They will say 'Luke sent them.' That's me. Fair enough?" They were thrilled. Occasionally, I would have to deal with a skeptic who would test me, but most of the time this worked like a charm.

I would then assess which of my friends would be the best match for those women and send them to the table. I earned a lot of favors in those days. I'm sure I was indirectly responsible for a few marriages and subsequent families.

I got to know many other great guys on campus while seeking out prime candidates for the girls in my care for the evening. If I were to notice what I thought was a sharp-looking guy, I would ask him if he were interested in meeting hot women. If I got an "Are you kidding?" I would tell my story that I met some babes who told me they wanted to meet interesting guys. Just go to the table and say, "Luke sent me."

Of course, if I met a woman who really stole my heart, I would look for the right moment to get her undivided attention and make a pitch for Yours Truly being someone she should get to know. That actually worked a surprising number of times. Ah, the good old days. I was fearless and expected that approach to work, and it did! I had to remind myself to have that attitude in other parts of my life. What's that line? "It worked so well, I quit doing it!"

Hot dog! It looked like I got a break. Ask and you shall receive. Several young bucks walked in who were obviously friends with the two who were chatting up Miss Southern California. Now was my chance while they were busy welcoming their buddies. It was now or never.

3

I looked at the gentleman sitting next to me and said, "Save my seat. If I'm not back in ten minutes, you can give my seat to whoever you want to sit next to."

He smiled then nodded. "Good plan."

I moved in her direction. My timing needed to be right. She was being reluctantly introduced by the two guys who didn't want to include any horny newcomers in their conversation.

Then my opening appeared. It felt like the clouds had parted and the sun broke through. Not bad for a crowded, dark bar. Both guys turned away to talk to their friends and she was left unattended.

"Excuse me." I was trying to be as innocent as possible. I didn't want her to feel any pickup energy. "Can I say something to you?"

"Of course, you can say something to me. I can't guarantee how I'll respond, though. I might have to ignore you." Her eyes sparkled.

"You haven't ignored me so far," I said with as much charm as I could possibly express.

"The night is young." There was a playful tone in her voice.

This gal was as fun to talk to as she was to look at! I could feel her presence right there with me. I gathered up my courage and rolled the dice. "I think we're supposed to talk."

"About what?" she invited.

Wow, she's letting this work. "The future," I said in my deepest, most galactic Carl Sagan voice.

"The future of what?" Another inviting question.

"The future of us," I said, knowing that could bomb.

"What makes you think we have a future?" She rescued me again!

"I'm not exactly sure. It's a feeling. It's hard to explain." I knew this was an even bigger risk, but it felt right. Women tend to like "take charge" guys more than super-nice, gooey guys. Most men would turn into goo around a woman this beautiful. That's why it was a risk to expose any uncertainty.

She could gently pull away here and still look good if she wanted to.

"So I heard the words 'feeling' and 'hard' in the same sentence." She lowered her forehead and raised her eyebrows. "Is this a sexual feeling we're having?"

Unbelievable! How do I respond to that? If I said no, I would be saying I didn't think she was sexy. If I said yes, I would look like every other goof who was desperately trying to get to first base. I had to go for it.

"Actually, the feeling is in my heart." I put my hand on my heart and imagined I was madly in love with her.

She didn't move. She didn't blink. She was right there with me. "You expect me to believe you feel something in your heart for me? We just met."

"You're right. We just met." I pulled back and agreed with her.

There was a silence that probably only lasted three seconds, but it felt like an eternity. Then she said, "All right honey, you have thirty seconds to convince me your heart's involved. Tell me why I should believe you?" She was challenging me, but I could tell she didn't want the conversation to end.

Meanwhile, one of the original chaps touched her arm and said, "Sophia, there is someone I'd like you to meet."

She held up her finger and whispered, "Give me a couple of minutes."

Here was my chance. I needed to stay centered, stay grounded. Her name was Sophia. I could have guessed that. I took a deep breath and listened for what I was supposed to say to this four-alarm siren.

She turned back to face me. "I'm listening," she said.

"Did you ever just know you are supposed to do something? I know it sounds a little corny." The first part I knew she would say yes to. Then I wanted to see how she felt about her intuition.

"Honey, you're up to bat. You need to swing away, not watch the first pitch!"

5

That was not what I expected. And that was a good sports analogy. This gal had it all. I had to regroup and not panic. I needed to stay calm and listen for the words. Dear God, please give me the words!

"I'm not sure I can explain it," I said with a sigh.

"Honey, if I were in your situation, I'd go for it. What have you got to lose?" She'd called me "honey" again and was encouraging me to go for it. I might be in love!

"I get intuitive feelings," I said. "I don't know where they come from but I've learned to trust them."

"Oh, so you think you're intuitive? Okay, I like intuition," she said cautiously.

"Do you remember the last time you went with your feelings?" I was hoping she would just answer the question this time.

"Yeah, it was horrible! I made a huge mistake and it took a lot of time and effort to clean up the mess I made!"

Oops, not the answer I'd hoped for. "That sounds more like emotion than intuition. Whatever you did that turned out so horrible, did it feel like a good idea at the time, or did it feel right at the deepest level?"

"Probably more in the 'good idea at the time' category," she said. "You're right, I was upset and should never have said anything. It would have been better if I had just kept quiet. Not something I do very well."

"That's one of the things I like most about you. You hang in there and keep talking. I think that's an admirable trait even though it might get you in trouble."

She nodded as she pondered my psychic compliment.

"I know it sounds like a pickup line," I said. "But I have a feeling that you and I are supposed to do something together tonight."

She looked at me very intently. She was sizing me up and getting ready to decide what to do with me. "Are you ready to put that intuition of yours to the test? Are you ready to prove to me that you're worthy of my time and energy?"

Wow, where did that come from? This was a no-nonsense, *take-no-prisoners* type. I needed to match her intensity.

"I've waited for this moment all my life," I said.

"All right, hotshot, I have some things to tell you. You need to listen carefully and decide if you want to play. You have one chance with me. If you answer the questions correctly, you and I have a future, one wrong answer and you never see me again. Capisce?"

The gentle flower had disappeared. I was now conversing with the Warrior Princess. She had my attention, and I liked the intensity. And with the way she looked, I had to see where this would lead. "Okay, I'm in. What's the question?"

"There's more than one question, and we're not going to do it here. It's too noisy. Meet me at this address in thirty minutes."

She handed me a manila business card with just her name, address and telephone number. *Sophia Forlani* was in gold script. The card seemed a little unusual. This couldn't be her business card. Or maybe it was. Maybe she didn't need to say what she did on her card. If you had met her, she's not someone you were going to forget!

"Can I drive you?" I offered.

"Thanks, but that won't work. What's your cell number?"

"310-555-1212."

She punched the number into her phone. "Do you have GPS?"

"I do."

"Use it. Don't be late. Thirty minutes starting now."

I started to think about all the things that could go wrong with this...

"How long will it take me to get there?"

"Fifteen minutes, tops," she said.

"And you promise me you're going to be there?" I was looking for a confirmation I wasn't on a wild goose chase.

She gave me the *You're gonna have to learn to keep up* look. "What does that intuition of yours tell you?" she said.

7

"Okay, good answer. I'll see you shortly."

"Ciao." She flashed her teeth into a smile and winked at me. That was all it took. I was committed.

As I was walking toward the door, I realized there was the possibility that this was all some kind of practical joke and I'd never see her again. Or that I was about to get ambushed and mugged in some remote parking lot. But that felt more like my protective, analytical mind trying to keep me from another disaster than an intuitive warning to stay away. Intuitively, this all felt right in a way I could not explain. I guess that was the real fun of it all. It felt right.

When I opened the door to the outside, the fresh coastal air and the quiet of the parking lot were a welcome transition from the noisy bar. All those people talking, laughing, yelling…and all of that on top of the music. I always found having a conversation in a noisy club difficult. But that was an amazing conversation I just had with Sophia from Heaven. Maybe that's why we were headed to a new location. She did say she wanted a quieter place to talk.

I got in my car and punched the address into the GPS. Looked easy enough. Steely Dan came on the satellite radio playing *Aja*, a favorite. That felt like a good omen. We shall see, I thought, we shall see.

2. The Challenge...

The address on the card read *520 Main Street, Venice Beach, California.* The number was above the door. It was a two-story Victorian mansion on the corner of Main Street and Windward. Someone was keeping the building and the surrounding area in good repair. Lights were on inside. There were a few steps and then an expansive porch in front of the main door. No doorbell. There was a welcome mat, nice touch for a business.

I pushed on the door. It opened into a majestic reception area with a twelve-foot ceiling and dark walnut crown molding that circled the room. There were four big retro brown leather chairs, an oversized antique coffee table, and a few magazines. In the back of the room was a wide enclosed counter. A high-tech Herman Miller office chair was ready for a receptionist behind the counter and a bank of filing cabinets filled up the back wall. The feel of the room was part hotel lobby and part dentist office.

"Anybody home?" I said. I really wanted someone to answer.

"Be right there. Make yourself comfortable." I recognized her voice coming from down the hall. I felt better. So far so good.

I sat and grabbed a copy of *National Geographic*, a timeless waiting room classic. I could catch up on what was happening in remote areas around the world. This edition was a couple years old, but it would be news to me. I didn't keep up with current events like I used to.

"Hey, you made it." She was catching her breath like she had hurried to get there. "Come on back." She motioned for me to follow her.

I was excited to be with her again. "So is this your business?"

"It's a lot of things," she said.

"What do you do here?"

"The company is called ASC, as in *ask* a question, except it's spelled A-S-C. It stands for Advanced Sales and Communication. We are a training company."

"Sounds interesting." There was a shift in the energy between us. Things had cooled a little. I suspected that I might be more excited than she was about the potential of what could happen that evening. This was feeling more like a job interview than the next phase of a romantic interlude. I decided not to jump to conclusions. Like she said, the night was young.

As we walked into a large conference room, she said, "Have a seat." She pointed to the chair she wanted me to take and sat at the end of the table next to me. "We can talk here. Everyone's gone home. It's just us."

I liked the sound of that. I found it pleasing and promising that she had no reservation about being alone with me. After all, we had only known each other for an hour.

"How was the drive?" she asked.

"Easy. I know the area. I live near here."

"Oh, that's right." She was thinking about something else. Then she looked at me more intently for a second with those cheerful chocolate-brown eyes. I was putty in her hands. "So where were we?"

"Great question." I was eager to pick up where we had left off. "Well, I said I had a feeling that you and I were supposed to talk. You said 'About what?' I said, 'The future.'"

"That's right, you get these feelings, but you're not sure where they come from."

"You challenged the source of my feelings. I said I could feel it in my heart." I stopped to watch her reaction.

"It's all coming back to me now," she said, nodding. "The last thing I remember asking you was if you were ready to put your intuition to the test and prove to me that you're worth my time and energy. Then I said you have one chance with me. If you answer the questions correctly, you and I have a future, but one wrong answer and you never see me again. Do you remember that part?"

"I do." I maintained my composure even though her directness caught me by surprise this time. I still liked it.

"Are you still up for this?" Her radar for what I was feeling was as good as any I had ever witnessed.

"I am," I said.

"One thing I would like to make very clear: I'm counting on you to trust your intuitive instincts in your interactions with me no matter what. I don't want you to ever do anything that doesn't feel right, regardless of what I say or how I feel. Will you promise me you'll do that?"

"I think I can do that." Her request seemed a little unusual.

"And you always have a way out with me. If at any point you start to feel this is too weird or you find yourself saying 'I don't want to do this anymore,' you can pull the plug without any explanation or discussion."

"If you decide to bail on *me*, can I ask for an explanation?" I asked.

"Sure, but I have the option not to give one." She paused and watched me for a second. "We good so far?"

"We're good," I said.

"How are you feeling about this conversation?" she asked.

I was careful not to give my answer too quickly. I could tell she was looking to see how accurate I could be. "I'm intrigued," I said after taking a second to check in with how I really felt.

"That's it, you're intrigued?"

"Yep. That's it for now," I said.

"You're a smart, confident guy. I like that. There is a lot I like about you. I actually know a lot about you. I'm sure that sounds ominous since we just met, but I want to be straight with you."

"I like straight." My mind raced. How does she know a lot about me? *Why* would she know a lot about me? What was there to know? I was a manager at a nightclub and dabbled in life insurance sales. I was not a Russian spy!

"I need to ask you for a favor before we go any farther," she said.

"Sure, fire away." No matter where this conversation went, my feelings for this gorgeous creature were already such that she could ask me for almost anything and I would probably say yes.

"I can't tell you much more unless you promise me you can keep certain things to yourself. What I'm about to tell you is actually classified at the highest level. You can't tell anyone. If you ever did tell anyone, I would deny that I ever told you anything. I would say you were crazy, and I would also get in a lot of trouble with my superiors. I have an identity that I have to maintain. If someone blows my cover, it takes an enormous amount of time and energy to regroup, and the potential for problems and losses is larger than you can imagine."

"Classified information? You have a cover? I feel like one of us has watched too many spy movies! Is this some kind of test to see how I will react?"

"Well, yes and no. There are a lot of tests coming your way. This is a test of whether you believe me or not. I swear to you, I'm not making this up."

"You promise?" The only words I heard in my head at this point were *Candid Camera*! Stay cool, I told myself, next question. "So what happens to me if I spill the beans? Not that I would. But you make it sound like maybe this might be out of my league." I wanted to know what I was getting into.

"Fair question. I'll answer it. Here's a yellow pad." She pushed the pad of paper toward me. "I can see you have a pen. Purple ink, is it?" She was teasing me.

"Yes, I got tired of getting black and blue." I watched for her response.

"I'll want to hear more about that later." She returned to a more serious tone. "Write down your questions as we go. I will answer them, but I have to do it in a certain order or this will take forever. You okay with that?"

"Sure, why not?"

"Write down the question you just had or you will lose track. I'm about to give you a lot to think about."

"Let's see, my question was?" My mind went blank.

"What happens to you if you 'spill the beans'?"

There was nothing wrong with her memory. I had better pay attention if I was going to keep up with this one!

"I made some coffee. Do you want some?"

"Sure, black." I wanted to keep it simple for her.

"You write down your questions, and I'll get the coffee. Be right back." She pushed herself away from the conference table and started for the door.

She said to write down your questions, plural, which implied more than one. I wrote down *What happens if I spill the beans?* And don't forget *How does she know so much about me?* Write that down. How about *What kind of gun does she carry?* Or maybe it's a phaser! Nothing would surprise me at this point. What I really wanted to know was her favorite position in the sheets. I had better not put that on the list just yet. I will want to carefully imagine the options, and I'm sure that will lead to more questions.

She was back with the coffee. I had to get my brain back in the conversation!

"One coffee, black." She glided into the room as the consummate hostess and carefully set the coffee down next to my yellow pad. "I see you thought of some more questions for me."

"I did indeed." I gazed at her alluring silhouette and quickly imagined some of the possible answers to my more intimate questions. She approached the whiteboard at the head of the room. She found a marker and then turned toward me. "What I'm about to tell you will shock and amaze you. You won't want to believe certain things. You will question how I could know what I know. I don't expect you to believe everything you hear right away. It takes time to develop trust. My hope is that you eventually find what I'm about to tell you becomes a source of inspiration. Shall we begin?"

"Umm...I've already felt some of those things you just mentioned and it sounds like there's more on the way."

"Lots more, and relax. There's more good news than bad news. Do I have your undivided attention?"

I nodded.

"I came to the bar to see if I could pick *you* up." She paused to make sure I understood what she had just said and for me to let it in.

"Un-be-lievable." The whole evening flashed through my mind.

"I knew you would be at *The Back Door*. My job was to see if I could get you to approach me and start a conversation. Phase two was to have you feel strongly enough about me that you would meet me here so we could continue a more serious conversation without the distractions of the bar.

"You passed the first test. Your timing was impeccable waiting for the right moment with the two guys I was talking to. You trusted your intuitive instincts to find a way to

14

approach me. You were gentle, charming and sincere. You were good." She had a twinkle in her eye like she was proud of me somehow.

I faked a smile and shook my head in amazement. I realized this dish had a lot more going on than I'd anticipated. I could tell she had more to say but wanted to make sure I was ready for the next round. It felt like we were dancing for the first time. She didn't want to move without me. I had many questions, but I was sure of one thing—it was a rush being with her.

"Then you trusted your intuitive instincts to come here even though I gave you a slim chance of succeeding with me," she continued. "I said, 'Give me the wrong answer to one question, and you'll never see me again.' Those are not good odds, but you didn't give that a second thought. You were up for the challenge. You decided I was worth the risk. So far you've been making me look good and you get big points for that."

I slowly bowed my head and smiled in silent response to her compliment.

"Something else important...I put out a signal that I wanted to connect with *you*. Not everyone feels that signal. Actually, most guys don't feel it. You do. You passed another important test. You don't qualify for what we need you to do if you can't get those telepathic messages from me. You and I need to be highly connected."

"Wait, did you say what *we* need to do?"

"I said I know a lot about you. Our recruiting team has been studying you for some time to determine if you qualify to work with us on a top secret project. You have shown aptitudes in the past that made us keep track of you and watch your progress. You impressed enough people that you got an invitation to the party. There's nothing evil or sinister about any of this, which you will see as you learn more. It's just the most effective way to find the right candidates for demanding and important work. Everybody wins in the long run, and you

15

could potentially have a major role if you decide this is a path you want to pursue." She looked at me like it was my turn to speak.

"Can we push the Pause button and have a couple shots of tequila just to loosen up a little?"

"Absolutely not!" she said through a big smile that turned into a laugh. Her laughing at my irreverence made the whole evening worth the time and effort no matter what happened after that.

"Maybe later. We have a long way to go before we can break out the champagne! And I can guarantee you I won't be drinking tequila. I have gotten into way too much mischief drinking that stuff. We can take a break in a little while. Let's keep going for now."

"Okay," I agreed with a tone of fake disappointment.

She smiled and then turned to the whiteboard. I made an important entry on my yellow pad: *Tequila, mischief, get details.*

Sophia was deep in thought. I decided to honor her silence. I suspected she was strategizing how she was going to tell me as much as possible in the shortest amount of time. I could tell she was a good coach. She knew how to tell me just enough to get the important points without overwhelming me with details.

"So here's the short version of what's happening. The Universe is much larger than most humans realize. There are more galaxies and planets than we can begin to comprehend.

"In our Milky Way alone, which is a relatively small galaxy, there are 400 billion stars. What people don't know is that over one hundred of those stars are planets just like ours that are inhabited by intelligent beings. Some are similar to humans, some are way more advanced. We don't have the technology to see them, let alone visit them."

"Time-out." I formed a *T* with my hands. "Sorry to interrupt, but I wouldn't be paying attention if I didn't ask.

How do you know this?" I pleaded with a hint of *please don't turn out to be an escaped mental patient!*

"That's an important question. Let me keep going and this will make more sense."

"All right."

"Space travel and all the power that goes with it is a privilege in the Universe, not a right. There is an evolutionary challenge before a species can have significant space travel, and it can be taken away. You have to prove that your kind can consistently operate from a peaceful, positive perspective. In other words, they don't give space travel to violent beings.

"Planets that have earned space travel don't have wars, poverty, crime or hunger, for starters. Disease is rare. It's a whole different reality when negativity and the survival mentality have almost no effect. Living in abundance while serving your community becomes a way of life, which is much easier if you're not consumed with trying to survive in a cruel world.

"There is a name for the jump or leap to the positive context and all the power that goes with it. They call it *lightspace*. When you reach a state of critical mass of the most positive human qualities, you become exponentially more capable of all kinds of things that would otherwise be impossible.

"You are familiar with *Star Wars*. That is what would happen if we gave space travel to just anyone. They would all be fighting each other for dominance of the Universe. The planets that have achieved lightspace decided that the less evolved planets would be isolated so they could not hurt anyone but themselves. Earth is a lower-level, isolated planet."

I really wanted to believe her but there was a voice screaming in my head, "This is a trap!" They could be trying to lure gullible young men into a lifetime of hard labor in a Russian gulag. I decided to cautiously go along for now. She was so hot.

"The part that amazes me the most is that so many planets are inhabited." I didn't want her to know I was having my doubts. "I always felt that was true. When I would look up at the stars on a clear night, I knew there was no way we were the only ones. I have always suspected we were on the lower end of the evolutionary curve. I heard someone describe Earth as the 'armpit' of the Universe. It made me angry, but I suspected it was probably true."

"So here's the deal," she said. "We are at a critical point, and time is running out. The folks in charge are saying 50,000 years is enough. If we can't achieve the shift to lightspace in the relatively near future, we get the final flush. Humans on planet Earth become extinct." She paused and looked at me intently before she continued. "The 7 billion souls who are alive on Earth right now—all die.

"We are not going to let it get to that point if I have anything to say about it!"

There was major *don't mess with me* energy in her words. I liked it. I couldn't think of anything I didn't like about her. Besides that, this story was getting more interesting by the minute. It was far-fetched, but there was a possibility that everything she had said was true.

Had we been brainwashed by well-meaning but clueless people who actually believed everything was fine? This wouldn't be the first time that had happened. Again, I decided to play along. "Okay. So how do we do it? How do we make the shift to lightspace?"

"Primarily by quieting your mind so you can hear the guidance of your more evolved, more intelligent self. Some call it your Higher Self, and it usually communicates through intuitive promptings. Some call it being guided by your soul rather than your intellect. Some describe it as being guided by an intelligence that comes from a connection with God rather than getting your directions from your survival-oriented ego. My favorite is simply you *go with your heart instead of your head*."

"I get intuitive visions about all kinds of things," I said, trying to figure out where I fit in all of this.

"I know." There was a tone in her voice that suggested she knew a lot about my intuitive ability. I decided to let that go for now. I had too many other questions that I hoped she would answer.

"Remember, I said you're going to have to make some big decisions in about an hour. We're getting close. But first let's take a short break. I need to pee and check my messages."

Sophia disappeared down the hall. I was having great fun with an eye on the prize. Her story was way out there, but people have crazy ideas about how we got here and why we are here. Whatever the story, I couldn't take my eyes off her! I wanted to see if I could get her into a more relaxed conversation that could lead in an intimate direction.

Then I heard a noise toward the front door. I went out into the hallway. "Is someone there?" I said. Strange, I thought I heard footsteps. I moved to check it out. As I got to the reception area, I saw the front door slowly closing. Someone had been in the office. What were they doing? Did they have a key? Were they stealing something? Or maybe they were watching us and listening to our conversation? Something didn't feel right.

3. Your Mission...

Ten minutes had passed. She walked back into the conference room with her cell phone to her ear saying goodbye to someone she obviously cared about.

Then all her attention was on me again. I was excited just to be in the same room with this dreamboat. Yeah, she was gorgeous, but there was something else. I couldn't quite put my finger on it. Maybe she *was* a little nuts and that's what made her so irresistible. A romantic savant built to seduce unwitting guys starving for female companionship. I hoped that wasn't the case. Oh well, I couldn't think of any place I would rather be!

"Okay, you ready for round three?" she said.

"Bring it!"

"This is where it gets a little more intense, because you get to choose if you want to be involved and at what level you want to play with us. Keep writing down your questions. We may have to answer some of them before you can make a final decision. Now let me ask *you* a couple of questions."

"Shoot."

"Have you ever felt like you had a calling?" she asked.

"Yes, I probably should have been a singer. I tell people I didn't want to live that lifestyle. I was actually too unsure of myself to take that risk so I chose something easier."

"How did you know you had a calling to be a singer?"

"My first memory of being noticed for my musical ability was about age thirteen. I had taken piano lessons for a few years. I could listen to the popular songs and figure out how to play them without any sheet music. I could play the keyboard parts to some of the more challenging songs. So I got invited to practice with the most popular rock band in my town and played the keyboard parts that I knew. Those were magical days.

"I kept at it and played in a couple of rock bands in high school. I have vivid memories of being on stage in front of packed gymnasiums pounding out my favorite songs. Being the center of attention as the lead singer was a rush I will never forget. The power of my voice and the impact it had on the audience astounded me. Looking back, I didn't understand how profound that experience was for me. Unfortunately, I was too scared of my own shadow to pursue a creative career."

"How would you describe the best feeling you can remember about being on stage singing your heart out?" she asked.

"It felt like I was home. And that was confusing because it didn't match who I thought I was supposed to be at the time."

"Describe the feeling of being home. Forget about the confusion."

"I can feel it right now sitting here. It was amazing."

"How did it feel? Give me more words."

"Let's see…home, power, impact, sound, loud, harmony, fun, friends, laughter, creative, special, popular, attention, pretty girls, and you know where that goes."

"Hmmm, I do. Your words are good. What were you thinking about when you were singing?"

"Not much. It was more about feeling and listening. I was focused on making the sound that was coming out of me match what I was feeling. I could hear what I wanted to sound like and just did it. It was fun, yet there was a challenge to it. The challenge was to really zero in on the feeling and nail it. I vowed to myself that no one was ever going to say, 'Can you do it one more time with feeling?' I tried to nail it the first time, every time."

"I can hear you nailing it. I can tell you have that ability to hear something and then perform it the way you hear it. That's a gift. Did you have stage fright?"

"Yes. I was always really nervous at the beginning of a performance. Most of that fear would go away after a few minutes. The music was so loud and penetrating, the sound and the rhythm took over and swept you away. Then once I started to sing, that was an addictive rush I couldn't get enough of."

"Sounds like you *were* really home!" she said.

"I was, but I didn't understand that at the time."

"You knew something special was happening. You just didn't realize how special it was."

"Right on." I was moved by the way she got what I was talking about. There was something indescribably sublime about performing in front of an audience that loved what you were doing.

"So here's the deal, sugar." Her voice was soft. Then she paused and looked directly into my eyes. She wanted my undivided attention. "There is so much to know about what we are doing here, it's almost endless. I don't have time to give you all the facts. I don't have time to give you a tiny fraction of the information your analytical mind wants before you make a decision to work with us. To some degree that's by design.

"We need people who can accurately access and follow their intuitive instincts, as if their life depended on it. If you don't think you can do that, or you're afraid you can't do that, we need to know that now. There is no dishonor in saying this is not for you. You would be helping us out by turning us down if this isn't right for you.

"Our experience has been that applicants who can't make the intuitive leap with some confidence at this stage don't make it in the program anyway. It is better to opt out now before we invest a ton of time and resources in you and then have you bail out. That really puts us behind, and we want to avoid that scenario at all costs.

"That being said, you know enough to be able to decide if you want to be one of the Knights of the Round Table. Let me give you the parameters of the offer so you can decide what you want to do. Listen carefully..."

She stopped talking and set her notes down. She looked at me for what seemed like a long time before speaking. "We want to help you achieve lightspace as quickly as possible so you can show others how to make the jump. We need a certain percentage of the population to break through to lightspace by a certain time in order for the whole planet to make the jump. Our goals are ambitious. Some would call them unachievable. But I think you are already getting a sense of how we like to play here."

I didn't know what to say, so I just nodded occasionally to let her know I was listening.

"We need you full-time as soon as possible. We will give you time to phase out your current employment, but we are under pressure to keep that short. You will be spending all your free time training.

"We pay well. Show us what you made last year and what you are averaging now per month. We have a formula that will almost double your current income the day you start. Once you make it to lightspace, you get a substantial raise and some other perks that I'm sure you'll like.

"You will answer to me as well as act as my partner. And here's the real meat of the commitment: you must be willing to trust me with your life and do whatever I ask you to do.

That level of commitment is standard procedure in the military. There is no difference here. We are not a division of the military, but it's the same commitment with the following stipulation, which is somewhat unusual.

"I will never expect you to do anything that does not feel right to you. However, if I ask you to do something and you *don't* do it, that is the end of the dance. You are instantly fired and returned to civilian status. There will be no discussion. We will not hear each other out and argue who is right or wrong. There will be no appeal hearing. We don't have time for any of that. If we don't make this work, what happens along the way is insignificant if we aren't going to be around to talk about it.

"We have no interest in trying to make this job feel right to you. It either feels right or it doesn't. You can pretend it feels right. You can delude yourself into thinking it feels right. You can rationalize that this is right for you. We emphatically request that you only take the job if it feels right at the deepest level.

"How are you doing with all this?" she said.

"It's a lot all at once. I have some concerns."

"One more thing. Not only does this offer need to feel right, I need the guy on the stage singing his heart out. I need you to give this everything you've got and then find some more to give after that. Are you capable of that level of commitment?"

"Sure, I'm willing to give it everything I've got. What's the downside?" I asked.

"You mean other than you could be mistaken for a government spy and be tortured or killed or put in some remote prison until they find out you really don't know anything!?"

"Could that really happen?"

"Actually, once you reach lightspace, the chances of you having any kind of horrible future disappear. Once you hit lightspace, you are protected in ways you can't imagine. And, we will do our best to keep you safe until then."

24

"I like the sound of that. But let's say I have to quit or get fired, what happens then?"

"Your memories of the program get erased," she said.

"That's somewhat radical. Am I a drooling idiot for the rest of my life?"

"That depends," she said more seriously. "Having your memories erased is an unpredictable process. We never know how that's going to turn out. You might not be able to go back to your old job if you don't remember anything about it. You might not remember important people in your life. Getting your memories erased should be considered a last resort. You most likely won't be able to go back to the life you had before."

"In the meantime, you're going to protect me so I'm not tortured or killed as a spy until I reach lightspace. Once I reach lightspace, I am protected somehow." I repeated her vow of protection to let her know that was important to me. "How long will it take?"

"That depends on you and your process, which we cannot predict."

"What if I give it 110 percent and I can't get to lightspace? Then what?"

"We know you have the aptitude to do it. You have more mental capability than most of those who have already made it. But with that big brain of yours comes baggage. Everybody has barriers. You may also have more barriers to contend with than the others.

"It's *possible* that you could *not* reach lightspace but not *probable*. If you have done your best and you are of value to the program, you will have a job. We are not going to fire you because you don't make lightspace. You just won't be able to be in the leadership position we are planning for you."

"How much time do I have to make the decision?"

"We want you to sleep on it. If you are who we think you are, we already know your answer, and so do you. But we still want you to sleep on it. If you wake up tomorrow and it feels right, you're a go."

"Will you answer more questions?" My folder of questions was getting to be the size of a small phone book.

"That depends on the questions."

"Can I ask you why you are doing this work?"

"This is what feels intuitively right to me at the deepest level. This is what I am called to do. This is what I was born to do."

"How do you know that with such certainty?"

"You just know, honey. It's not something you figure out."

"Tell me again why lightspace is so important," I asked.

"Lightspace is a higher, positive reality. In our current reality, our attachment to negativity keeps us stuck. We can't grow beyond a certain point. There are over one hundred wars in progress right now as we speak. More than 50 million will die this year from disease. More than 25,000 died today from starvation, and it'll happen again tomorrow. We are destroying our ecosystem. The day is coming when you'll have to wear a mask and protective suit just to go outside!"

I knew all that was true. My life was challenging enough without thinking about all the things that didn't work about this world. I wanted to make a difference. I wanted to lessen the suffering of people. But I didn't feel like I had the power to do anything about any of it.

Then her eyes lit up and a big grin appeared on that pretty face. "And the good news is—*drum roll please*—all that negative stuff goes away when we jump to lightspace. No more wars, no more starvation, most diseases disappear, and Earth is restored to its pristine state in a relatively short amount of time. Most importantly, we find ways to care for our people and our planet that we could only dream about before lightspace!

"Also extremely important is the physical transformation. Traveling through space at the speed of light is very demanding on the physical body and requires the ability to maintain a higher cellular vibration. If you repeatedly travel at lightspeed without achieving the higher vibration of lightspace, you age much faster and have increased health problems. So there is major motivation for achieving lightspace and maintaining it from both a universal travel perspective and your own personal health and well-being. The benefits of lightspace both physically and mentally are sensational and a favorite topic of mine, which we will have to continue at another time."

She was deep in thought for a few seconds and then smiled again. "The most amazing part is when you can travel at lightspeed, you can go anywhere in the Universe you want to go. The Universe is so beautiful and so diverse and so much damn bigger than you ever imagined. There are so many choices that you have to be in a transformed state just to maintain your sanity. We like to say, 'It's bigger than big.' You can't really describe it to anyone. You have to see it to believe it."

"So you have traveled to other planets?" I had to ask.

"I can't answer that question until you have a clearance level. I could get in a lot of trouble."

"Come on, I can keep a secret."

She thought for a second.

"There is so much I want to tell you, but I can't yet."

"Are you human?"

"Don't I look human?"

"You look *out of this world* to me, babe. How about sex?"

"Easy there, big fella."

"I mean, how is the sex once you reach lightspace?"

Her face flushed for a second then she quickly recovered. She had an impish smile that revealed I had touched a nerve, but she didn't want me to know. "That is definitely a discussion for *later*."

"Come on, I'm a healthy, horny guy. Give me something to look forward to!"

She stood up from her chair and raised her arms into a big stretch. "It's getting late. You've had quite a day. Can you find your way home?"

That stretch was an inspiration. There was something about a voluptuous woman with her arms in the air that put me in the mood for love. But I didn't want to blow it either. She was saying good night. "So what's next?"

"Meet me here for coffee, 8 a.m. sharp."

"I'll be here."

"You understand you can't talk about any of this with anyone," she warned. "If you do, they won't let you keep your memories of me. I know that sounds hard to believe, but you have to trust me. This is the big leagues. They can do almost anything at the push of a button. Besides, no one would believe you anyway!

"I want you to make the right decision for yourself. I don't want you to do this if it doesn't feel right down to your toes.

"I want you to be able to look at me and smile no matter what happens. In one version of the story, when you see me again and you try to pick me up like before, I will gently turn you down. In the other version of the story—the one I'm rooting for by the way—the next time you see me, I am the greatest partner you will ever know in the biggest game ever played."

"That's an intriguing perspective. How about a hug?" I really wanted to touch her.

She put her arms around my neck. "You're dangerously cute."

I felt love, warmth, tenderness, and power all at the same time. The only thing I could think to say was, "Thank you for tonight."

"You're welcome. I understand how you feel. I've been where you are." She gave me a gentle squeeze then slowly pulled away.

As we walked down the hall toward the front door together, she said, "Don't worry about thanking me. This is the most

28

demanding work you will ever do. You will earn whatever you get out of this deal. And if you make the choice to do it, I guarantee it will be beyond anything you have ever imagined.

"You have to look inside to see what your heart really wants. There's the life you thought you would live with an occasional adventure. Now there's a new option on the table where adventure and the unknown become a way of life."

She opened the front door and stepped outside. "Nice night."

"Looking at the stars will never be the same," I said, acknowledging her story. The look I got back was a reserved smile that said *you have no idea*. I was intrigued.

"See you at eight," she said. "Get some sleep."

"Hasta mañana." I waved goodbye to Miss Universe as I walked to my car. I had met the most dazzling woman I had ever seen and she liked me. She told the most outrageous story about the world coming to an end if we don't obtain this positive state of mind called lightspace. And that there is intelligent life on other planets in our galaxy that have space travel. Was it possibly true that only a privileged few were aware of what was really going on? Was I about to become one of the few who knew?

Or was she delusional? She said so many things that would qualify her as committable, yet she spoke with such clarity and conviction. What do I do now? Do I disappear into the night and try not to think about her? Good luck with that. Or do I go back tomorrow and see what's next? I needed sleep.

When I got to my car the passenger door was unlocked. I was obsessive about locking my car since I had my stereo stolen last year. Not that locking the car was going to keep out a good thief, but it kept out the lazy ones. I looked around inside the car and nothing seemed to be missing. Why would someone break into my car and not take anything? What were they looking for? That was the second time tonight I had the unsettling feeling that something dark was watching me.

4. The Enrollment...

Meditation gongs were gently announcing a new day. I reached to turn off the alarm on my cell. I was awake but I didn't sleep like I usually do. I was having a dream about not having enough time to study for a college final, and I kept having that same short dream over and over. That probably wasn't a good sign.

Somehow, I got ready for my 8 a.m. meeting with Sophia. As I pulled up to the building, all the spaces were taken on the street. I'd have to park behind the building. There were a lot of cars that were not there yesterday. That made me feel better. Analytical Guy and Worried Guy inside my head were envisioning being eaten alive by an unkillable mutant alien. I wanted to be the picture of confidence and resourcefulness to my arresting new love interest, but I was an emotional wreck.

I walked into the grand reception room. This time there was someone watering the plants. "Hi, I'm Candy. Can I help you?" Tall, tan, streaked highlights in her golden brown hair, she had to be a former cheerleader. She was about twenty-five with that fresh-faced, innocent look. A short skirt, knee socks and designer bowling shoes accented her long, graceful legs that had the muscle tone of an Olympic swimmer. The look really worked for her, and for me too.

"I'm Luke Lamaire here to see Sophia Forlani."

"Hi, Luke. Is she expecting you?"

"I sure hope so." I blurted out a nervous laugh.

"Oh, you're the new guy. Sorry, she said she had a meeting but I didn't realize it was with a really cute guy." Her face got a little color after she realized what she had said.

"Thanks, Candy. You're pretty cute yourself."

"Don't tell her I said you were cute." Her embarrassment was seductive.

"That'll be our little secret," I said.

"Thanks, Luke. I'll tell her you're here." She disappeared around the corner.

Sophia walked in. "Luke, good morning!"

Ah, the soothing voice of the siren. She was a vision in precisely fitted black pants, black heels, and a soft natural silk top with a simple gold necklace and bracelet. The cut of her blouse was going to be a pleasant distraction. I'd rather have the view than not have it. "Sophia," I said with a slight bow.

"Did you sleep?"

"Like a rock."

"Good for you. I like a man who can relax under pressure." She motioned for me to follow her down the hall.

"I think 'passed out' is probably a better description."

That got a short laugh. She turned into the kitchen and waved me in. "What would you like? We have fresh coffee, herbal tea, several kinds of juice, bagels, toast, croissants, granola, fruit, yogurt... Help yourself."

"What a spread. Breakfast is my favorite meal. I think I'll just stay in here all day!"

"I think we have other plans for you. Get whatever you want and come sit with me on the patio."

I was starving. I hadn't had any time to think about food since yesterday afternoon. I needed a strategy. I would toast a bagel to buy time and eat a croissant while I waited. Then I would finish with a few quick pieces of fruit and yogurt before I made my appearance on the patio. I would save the bagel and coffee for the table and maintain the appearance of a light eater.

I finally wandered out onto a spacious patio with lots of potted plants, a small fountain that babbled away, and a big green canvas canopy that was providing shade. There was oversized wicker furniture with bright floral cushions, a resort favorite. I carefully placed my bagel and coffee on the table next to her and sat down.

"Is that all you're having? You'll have to go back for more." I got the impression that abundance was a theme around here, which I liked.

She was rustling through a local newspaper. Then she put it down and looked at me. "So how are you feeling?"

"I'm good. I'm intrigued with the possibility of working with you. I am moved by the importance of the work you are doing. I'm a tad apprehensive about all the unknowns. It's a challenge to feel confident when you don't know exactly what will be included in your job description."

"Good answer. That's exactly where you're supposed to be right now. Let me ask you the other important question." She waited for me to respond.

"Sure."

"Did this job feel right to you last night before you left?"

"*You* feel right to me. The idea of the job is an interesting one, but as we have discussed, I have a lot of questions. I think I would need to know more about the job to know if it feels right."

"How did you feel about the job this morning?"

"About the same. I'm here because you feel right to me. The rest of it is a blur."

"That was not quite the answer I was hoping for, but I will honor your concerns. I assume you have some questions."

I opened my portfolio, which was full of notes from last night, and I had jotted some things down I wanted to cover.

"Okay, so even though we've just met, one of the big reasons this job feels right to me is being able to work with you. My concern is that you're a recruiter. I connect with you, I sign up with you, and then I rarely get to see you or work with you."

"Fair enough. I *am* a recruiter, and I'm recruiting you for my own team. I'm looking for key players I will personally train and maintain a close relationship with until the end of this assignment. The specifics of what we do together will depend on your aptitudes and skill level.

"You and I will do a lot together, and I am looking forward to that. I like you. We are a lot alike. But this isn't just you and me against the world. I'll admit that sounds romantic, but that model isn't big enough for the monster we must face.

"And let me add something you will find different here. There are a lot of gifted, wonderful people involved in this project. If you're as good at this as I think you'll be, you're going to get invitations to work with other groups. You make a commitment to the program but not necessarily to only one group.

"We operate at our peak to the degree we are doing what feels intuitively right. That means you and I work together because it feels right to both of us. If that changes for either one of us, we have to honor that and move on without missing a beat. We have to trust what we are guided to do and not let our emotional attachments slow us down from doing what needs to be done. Attachment is a big reason why Earth has not made the leap to lightspace!"

"I get it now. That was a better answer than I expected. I think I'm in love... If I'm in love with you, will that affect my ability to do this job?" I could feel a rush of confidence coming back.

"It better not!" She rolled her eyes. "That's the whole point! I need you to do what feels right no matter how you feel about me or anyone else, for that matter. Do I have your word on that!?"

"You do."

"All right then." She breathed a quiet sigh of relief and there was a hint of a smile peeking through that she didn't want me to see. I did just say I was falling in love with her.

She liked it when I got her riled up. My experience was that women like to feel tension more than men. Teasing women in a way that makes them a little insecure or making outrageous requests or just telling them what to do actually feels good to them. I wanted that to be part of my job description—*make Sophia feel good*—although I doubted I would ever see it in writing.

"What's next on the list?" she asked.

"Okay, you are used to being undercover and dealing with top secrets. That's all new to me. What do I tell my family and friends? I'm assuming this isn't like the witness protection program where I get a new identity, go to some remote location, and never see anyone I used to know." I was joking, but I hoped that wasn't true.

"Of course, you get to keep your relationships with your family and friends. You can talk about our sales and communication training but not anything classified. Sometimes family and friends ask too many questions, and that can make it harder to spend time with them. If they keep asking a lot of questions, it gets old.

"We will prepare you to deal with this issue. Most people put in enough effort to maintain the relationships that are important to them. At the same time, they tend to *limit the visits* because it's easier on everyone that way.

"Anyway, with the intensity and demands of this job, you aren't going to have much free time until you get good at our job. You're going to be busy, and you'll enjoy the pace because of the rewards and what's at stake. Feeling like you are making an important difference in the world is a powerful motivator.

"And you're going to make lots of new friends who will become a new family. You will feel an instant connection.

Your new family will grow and be big before you know it. Who you get to work with is a big perk in this job."

"How about the transition into the job?" I asked.

"We will make that seamless. We will help you make the transition, and as I mentioned before, you will have the money you need to live your current lifestyle. We don't want you worrying about where the money is coming from. We need 110 percent of your focus and energy to learn this job as fast as possible."

"That sounds almost too good to be true. No one has ever told me they didn't want me to be concerned about money. That is somewhat remarkable."

"So are you. That's why you're here."

"Thank you." That felt good. I sure hope this wasn't a mistaken-identity thing. I wondered if I had a double in L.A.

"Also, don't make any changes in your current job situation until we talk more. We may be able to use the work you are doing as part of your training and your cover. We don't want to draw any undue attention to you. So, for now, we will work around your schedule. Take as much time off as you can to train with us."

I nodded slowly. What was wrong with any of that? I asked myself.

"What's your next question?" she said.

"What's the biggest reason agents don't make it? You must have blowouts. I need to know how that works and how I can avoid it."

"Yes, it's rare, but there are blowouts. We try to minimize this by being as careful as we can with our selection process, but sometimes we miss things. Sometimes things happen that are totally out of anyone's control. This can be a dangerous business. Those situations are difficult. We try to learn from our mistakes so we can prevent repeating them in the future."

"So what is the number one reason for failure?" I asked.

"Negativity."

"Say more."

"Maybe I should say 'a negative vision.' When someone creates a negative vision about something or a negative thought—and I should include a negative feeling about something—that's when the trouble starts. If you continue to give energy to a negative vision, negative thought or negative feeling, something negative is going to happen. Also, negative things by definition *take away* from what we have."

"Give me an example."

"What sports do you play?"

"All of them at one time or another."

"What's one that you're not as good at?"

"Racquetball."

"Why not?"

"There are a couple of basic shots I find hard to hit well, and I don't like being cooped up in the little room. I like space."

"So what decision did you make about racquetball?"

"That I didn't like it enough to want to keep playing."

"So you made a negative decision about racquetball. You now have negative thoughts and feelings about racquetball. So if someone calls you and says, 'Hey, let's play racquetball,' what are you going to say?"

"Probably, 'No thanks.'"

"Okay, so your negative decisions have now created a preference against racquetball which takes racquetball out of your life. Remember, negativity takes something away.

"Let's go for a more intense example. Is there anything you're afraid of?"

"Sure, I hate walking on beams high up in the air on construction sites."

"You have done that?"

"A few times. The worst was one time I was on a construction site after everyone had gone home. I took the elevator up ten floors, and the elevator broke. My choices were to stay up there all night until the guys came back the next morning or I could walk a hundred feet across some beams and get to another elevator. I have excellent balance if I am moving like with ice hockey or snow skiing, but if I'm standing still, looking down ten floors, it scares the bejeebers out of me."

"What did you do?"

"I walked the beams, and I hated every second of it! That was as scared as I have ever been. I swore I would never do anything like that again."

"Why didn't you just find a spot to rest until the guys came back the next day?"

"There wasn't anyplace safe enough to rest. I was afraid if I fell asleep I would forget where I was and fall to my death."

"How about the elevator? Why didn't you just stay in that?"

"When I got out of the elevator, the door jammed so I couldn't get back in."

"Great story! So what were you afraid of?"

"I didn't think I would feel very good if I fell ten floors." I thought the answer to that question was a bit obvious, but I loved the attention I was getting. I was growing very fond of this supermodel asking me questions and decided not to give her a hard time.

"Have you been seriously injured before, broken bones?"

"Four or five times, all sports related."

"So why are you afraid of getting hurt?"

"Because it's painful and takes a long time to recover."

"So does your knowledge that you could fall to your death or that you could get seriously injured and take forever to heal keep you away from walking on beams high up in the air at construction sites?"

"I don't even get close to those beams."

"That's how you blow out of this program. Something negative happens to you that you can't recover from mentally. You make a decision that it's just too painful to do it again. Or your fear is so intense, you're paralyzed at the thought of returning to duty."

"So that's the downside," I said quietly.

"Next question," she said.

"I have been involved in a number of things in my life where I was made a lot of promises about how great the job was going to be, and though there were some good parts, it was never quite as good as they made it sound. There were parts they didn't tell me about because they didn't want me to quit before I gave it a try. We've been having our own version of that discussion. I know there are always difficult and hard parts of any job. But it sounds like some of the perks of this job are better than usual. We have talked enough about the downside. Tell me more about the upside."

That got the biggest smile I had seen in a while.

"I thought you'd never ask," she said playfully. "Well, let's see. Can you remember when you were a little kid and you got really excited? So excited that you peed your pants? I'm just talking about a little bit, not a major disaster. Other people wouldn't even notice."

"I'm not sure I remember that right off the top of my head, though I'm sure it probably happened somewhere along the way." I wasn't exactly sure where she was going with this.

"I feel like I've gotten out on a limb here. Maybe this happens to girls more than it does to guys. Anyway, it has happened to me more times than I would like to admit. I'm a little embarrassed that I even brought it up. But since I did, let me see if I can finish what I was trying to say."

"Please." I was doing everything I could to keep a straight face.

"This is the best job in the Universe if you really want to make a positive difference. You will learn ten times more in this job than any other. There will be people with tears in their eyes thanking you for all you've done for them. They will say that meeting you was the most important thing that ever happened to them. You will make more lifelong friends in this job than you will ever have time for. How am I doing so far?"

"Sounds great."

"And yes, this job is challenging. There will be days you will wonder if you can go on, and you will. There will be days you feel like quitting, but you won't. The good stuff is too good. Just like any job, there are parts that are routine and boring, and sometimes you feel if it goes any slower you're going to explode.

"But then there are the good times, the fun times, the times that make it all worthwhile. Where you get to go places and do things that you could not now imagine if you tried! And those, my friend, are what makes it all worth it!"

"I think I hear crowd noise," I said. "Yes, you're getting a standing ovation from the spirits of past agents."

"Oh Lord, what have I done? I can hear it now. My partners will be asking the new recruits, 'Did Sophia give you the pee-your-pants speech yet?'"

"We can keep the pee-your-pants part just between you and me if you like," I said. I wanted to honor her willingness to be open and vulnerable with me.

"Thank you," she said.

I was tempted to say, "You look relieved," but decided even though that was a creatively brilliant thing to say, she was ready to move on.

"I have to run to a meeting," she said. "Can you do dinner tonight?"

"I would like that."

"I'll have Candy make reservations and text you the info."

"I'll be there."

"Ciao."

I took a walk to stretch my legs and think about what had just happened. I liked her answers. She clearly knew what she was doing. The words rolled off her tongue, but was she speaking from experience or just saying well-rehearsed lines? Logically, there was still the possibility that this was all a ruse. If the program was a sham, she was the best liar I had ever seen. Still, I needed to be sure. There had to be a way to get some proof that the program and everything she said were real.

My attraction to her was stronger than I had ever felt for a woman. I didn't want my infatuation to be the cause of my demise somehow. I wanted to follow my feelings for her, but I didn't want to end up looking like a fool either. Been there, done that. Love can make a woman appear to be flawless, and you talk yourself into doing things you would never do under ordinary circumstances.

I had walked in a big circle and was back standing by my car. I turned my head toward the sound of car engines whining and revving at high speed behind me. A black car was blocking a white car from passing by swerving back and forth. Then I heard a loud screeching sound and saw smoke coming from the tires of the black car as the driver slammed on its brakes in front of the white car. The white car tried to stop and then veered to the right at the last second to avoid colliding. As I stood next to my precious Beemer, the white speeding weapon smashed into the back of my car, collapsing the trunk and the backseat like a pancake in a split second. The shock of the crash and the flying glass pushed me backwards. I instinctively put my arms in front of my face as I realized what had happened, but I could already feel pieces of glass cutting my face as I fell backwards.

There were people everywhere within seconds asking me if I was all right. A fat fella with a commanding voice kept shouting, "Stand back! Give him some room to breathe." I liked that guy. He was having his fifteen minutes of fame.

Then I recognized Candy's face. She had a concerned look and was saying something to me but I couldn't understand her. She seemed out of place to me somehow. Then she was taking my blood pressure. Then I heard her say, "His vitals are good. He has a nasty bump on the back of his head that's going to need stitches. Sir, can you hear me? Sir, what's your name?"

I looked back at Candy. "You know my name. It's Luke."

"I know it's you, but I have to ask you that." Then it was like she went back into character. "Well, hi, Luke. Can you tell me how many fingers I'm holding up?"

"Two."

"Good," she said. "Do you know where you are?"

"Venice Beach."

"Right again. Luke, the guys are going to take you to the hospital to make sure you're okay. You hit your head pretty hard when you fell and you need some stitches. You're a lucky guy, Luke. Do you know how lucky you are?"

"Yes. But Candy, what are you doing here?"

"I was trained as an EMT. When I saw it was you, I asked the driver if I could examine you. He's a friend. I used to ride with him. He said to go for it. He's right here, you want to meet him? John, this is my friend Luke."

"Hi, Luke. Candy seems to think you're going to be okay but we need to take you to the hospital for some stitches and some tests. What do you say, you ready to go for a ride?"

"Sure." I looked back at Candy. "Thanks. You'll have to tell me more about what just happened later."

"I'm glad you're all right," said Candy. "See you soon." She kissed her hand and then touched my forehead with it.

She was a sweetie but I had a feeling there was something she wasn't telling me. Oh well, on to fun and games at the hospital.

As I was riding in the ambulance, thoughts dashed through my mind. The whole event seemed strange to me. Several things didn't feel right—how Candy got there for one, and I remember seeing the driver of the white car as his black-tinted windshield shattered. He was wearing a full shoulder harness like the stunt drivers use. Then they got the driver out of the car and into the ambulance really fast and raced off. Too fast. It was almost like the ambulance was waiting around the corner for the dude to have an accident. Was it possible that this accident was staged? Was this an insurance scam? Was

Sophia involved somehow? I had a monster headache, and the painkillers they gave me were taking their toll. I concluded I was probably imagining things and let the drugs do their work.

5. Intuition 101...

I opened the sliding glass door to my balcony to let in some fresh air. I didn't feel like doing much after spending hours at the hospital. They let me go home if I would come back tomorrow for a couple more tests. They said I seemed to be okay, but they wanted to make sure. Sounded like a good idea. I was moving slower than normal, and my head was sore. They had given me some medication for the pain which I had not taken. I took a couple of Advil instead. The stronger pain pills made me too drowsy.

My mind wandered to Sophia and my potential new job on *Team Save the Planet*. I knew so little about what I'd be doing, but the idea of having smart coworkers who had the resources to make things happen and getting paid well to do it sounded like an ideal job, no matter what the objectives were.

My phone rang. Sophia was calling. I wondered if she sensed I was thinking about her.

"Hey, Luke here," I answered.

"Luke, Sophia. My God, are you okay? I just heard what happened. I was at a meeting that went long and my phone died. I am so sorry I wasn't able to be with you at the hospital."

43

"That's okay. You didn't miss anything. It was all pretty boring."

"Are you in pain?"

"I fell backwards and hit my head. I have a really hard head so the damage was minor." She seemed to miss my attempt at some humor.

"I'm so sorry this happened to you and I'm so glad you're okay."

"Thanks. A few feet closer to the curb and I would've been a goner. I've had hours to sit and reflect this afternoon. I've definitely reevaluated what's important to me. This kind of thing is a reminder that your life can be taken in a blink. We forget we're not here forever."

"I'd like to talk to you more. Do you feel well enough to still do dinner?"

"Sure, I'm going stir-crazy sitting around here. Everybody is acting like I shouldn't do anything, but I feel fine."

"I will have Diego pick you up in the limo and take you to the restaurant."

"You have a limo?" I said.

"We have a lot of things you don't know about." She laughed.

"I'm impressed."

Diego drove up in a pristine black limo and texted me. He was a quiet Hispanic man in his mid-thirties who obviously spent time in the gym. Making small talk was the last thing I wanted to do, so I was glad Diego didn't feel a need to entertain me. I will admit I felt pretty important being picked up in a limo and hoped the neighbors noticed. An ambulance ride and a limo ride in the same day. What's next, a helicopter ride to the airport and then a private jet to Paris?

The name of the restaurant was Midori, like the Japanese melon liquor. Center stage was a big sushi bar with five sushi chefs carefully slicing and creating edible works of art. A couple of rows of small tables circled the men in black. On the sides of the room it was darker, except for the soft light flowing from huge aquariums that covered the outside walls. Along the back were private, enclosed booths.

"Irasshaimase!" Three chefs at the sushi bar simultaneously announced my entrance with their loud, friendly welcome. I bowed my head in acknowledgment. What a great custom. Don't just quietly welcome your patrons for the evening, let everyone in the restaurant know you just walked in the door!

"May I help you, sir?" said an elegant teenage Asian hostess. She was beautifully dressed in a brightly colored geisha kimono with impeccably pulled-back hair and white makeup.

"Reservation for Forlani," I said.

"The lady waits. Me take you." She bowed and gestured for me to follow her.

I didn't see Sophia anywhere as we started to walk, so I figured she must be hidden in the back somewhere. We eventually came upon two rows of private booths and walked toward the end. It was really quiet for a restaurant. There were pairs of shoes outside the dimly lit booths, but I could only see the silhouettes of people because of the sheer curtains.

The hostess pulled back a curtain, and there was Sophia in all her splendor. She sat on a cushion in bare feet. She had changed into a soft orange jumpsuit with a necklace made out of beads of dark wood. If I had to give the look a name, I would have called it "sporty elegant." Her cell was on her ear, and she was writing in her daybook. I smiled and waved. I got the "one minute" signal and then she pointed to where she wanted me to sit.

As I climbed into the booth, I heard the voice of our young hostess, "Take shoes off, thank you."

I complied and made myself comfortable. I liked sitting on a raised floor with cushions around a low table as long as I had back support. I found some. I liked this place so far.

"What would you like to drink?" said our stunning hostess in precise English.

45

"What's she having?" I pointed to the drinks on the table.

"Hot saké."

"Same-same." I tapped my fingers on my chest to indicate I wanted saké too.

The hostess bowed and vanished.

After a couple of minutes, Sophia finished her call. "Sorry, that was a fire I had to put out."

"No problem."

"So you're okay…I can see you got some cuts on your face. Do they hurt?"

"Only when I look in the mirror. I may end up with some new character in my face when this is all healed up."

"Scars can be sexy," she said.

"I hope so."

"You ready for some delicious food and great conversation?"

"I am. And I'm glad to be here with you. The nurses were cute at the hospital, but I like looking at you better."

"You haven't lost any of your charm. I'm just so glad you're okay. You could have been killed."

"Yeah, like I said before, I've done a lot of reflecting today. Some of the things that I thought were important this morning are not as important now."

"Can you give me a for instance?"

"Sure. I've spent a lot of energy trying to keep my life in control and trying to limit any big surprises. I now feel like a lucky guy and that maybe I've been spared for a reason. That was no accident today, so to speak. Maybe the Universe is trying to get my attention. I need to be more serious about what you've told me and be more serious about my potential role. I have to tell you that at first I thought you might be an escaped mental patient, however, a very attractive one I'd like to add."

"Yeah, go on!"

"Everything you were saying sounded more like the plot to a sci-fi movie than a possible reality. It was a shock to the safe little world I had put together and had complete control over."

"It's a shock to everyone who learns the truth. Don't feel like the Lone Ranger. It is such a shock to most people we need to keep it quiet. We don't want folks to become alarmed and make things worse. We need time to find and train the right folks to solve the bigger problem."

"So why do you think I'm qualified for this job?"

"A lot of what I see in you is more about who you can become. You don't automatically become who you can be without putting in the effort. You have to learn how to be at your best. You have the aptitudes and other strong indicators that say you can do it if you decide to go for it."

"Can you give me some traits you think I have that are key to the job?"

"Sure. You have made a lot of progress on your own. You're smart—gifted smart—so you learn really fast. You have access to your intuitive instincts, which we will help you develop even more. You have a good heart. You care about people deeply even though you may not always show it. You are open to new ideas and new technology. You are fearless in many ways, which we need in our leaders. And you have issues you need to work through to achieve lightspace just like the other leaders. Let's not forget you have a good connection with me on a telepathic level, which you proved last night with flying colors."

"I think we should begin all our meetings this way." I poured myself another cup of saké.

"I'll bet you do." She knew I liked what she had just said.

"So would you like to hear what I think about *you*?" I asked.

"Oh dear." She had the *what have I gotten myself into now* look. "Sure, why not? Fire away…just be gentle." A nervous smile covered up some apprehension about what might happen next.

"Well, let's see..." I pretended to be thinking really hard. I opened my portfolio so I would have something to write on. I was drawing this out as long as possible to add to the drama. The longer I waited, the more it looked like I was having a hard time thinking of anything to say. The tension was exquisite.

"Oh, come on! I think you're enjoying this too much!" She had to break the silence.

"You're right. I'm teasing you. I want to say this right... I have only known you a short time. Every bone in my body is telling me you are the most amazing woman I have ever met. You are smart, beautiful, loving, caring and kind. You obviously have tremendous abilities to be in the position you're in. Highly influential people have given you huge responsibility. You are keeping track of a large workforce and keeping things on schedule. You're a savvy recruiter and a phenomenal promoter. And probably most important, I love your outfits! And that's just for starters!" I paused to take a sip of saké.

"Unbelievable," she said, shaking her head. "So does this mean you're going to propose? Do you have the ring?"

We laughed hysterically. The saké was working.

As the energy settled a bit, I said, "I meant everything I just said. Most importantly, I'm glad to have you as a friend."

"Thank you. I feel the same."

I raised my saké cup. "Cheers to you and me."

She raised her cup. The audible clink confirmed our feelings for each other.

"We should order," I said.

"Oh, that's right, we're having dinner." She pretended to have totally forgotten about dinner, she was having so much fun.

I told Sophia to order for me. I knew she would make superb choices. One other surprise was the amount of energy I felt just being around her. When I had felt the surge of energy before, I thought I was just excited to be hanging out with

48

such a babe, but there was definitely something else happening. Being in close proximity to her was like being connected to a giant battery that gave off constant positive energy. There were times when it was so strong it was like a high. I couldn't help but wonder what it would be like to be holding each other naked... Come back, I told myself, come back to dinner with Sophia!

With ordering out of the way, she wanted to get down to business. She loved being playful and having fun, but she was driven. The mission was always close at hand. I'm sure that's why they had given her the job.

"How would you define intuition?" she asked.

"Big subject. Let's see. 'Internal promptings barely caught in the web of human consciousness.'"

"I like that," she said.

"The barely audible voice of Heaven."

"I really like that one. Where do you get these!?" she said, a little envious.

I gave my best Schwarzenegger impression. "*Total Recall*."

"Yeah, right." She didn't believe I had total recall, but the smile she was trying to hide told me she liked my Arnold impression. "So what else can you tell me about intuition?"

"Probably the most interesting thing about intuition is that you can't control it and you don't know when you're going to get the answer to your question. You have to be able to ask yourself a question and then let go of trying to figure out the answer.

"Also, the intuitive answer is usually not related to any other train of thought. Sometimes I will have an intuitive thought like 'Call John and Mary Walker.' I will ask myself if I was thinking about anything related to John and Mary. If the answer is no, it's most likely an intuitive message floating into my awareness and I have learned to pay attention to those!"

"Is there a difference between intuition and emotion?"

I figured she knew the answers to these questions but wanted to hear what I had to say on the subject. "Yes, and

49

most people don't make this distinction. Intuition is a quiet sense of knowing something is right or not right. Emotion is a more intense feeling based on a past experience that peaks and dissipates quickly. Intuitive feelings are slow to change. If something feels intuitively right today, it will feel right tomorrow and most likely for a long time after that."

"So intuition is a quiet sense for you," she said.

"Yes."

"How do you access your intuition?"

"I ask questions. It's like as soon as I ask a question, a bunch of little guys running around in my head are doing everything they can to find the right answer. Then when they get it, they float the answer out into my awareness hoping I'm paying enough attention to hear the answer. I know those little guys get frustrated with me because I don't always hear their answers."

"Hmm. I like your little guys," she said. "What kinds of questions do you ask your intuition?"

"That's the million-dollar question with such a simple answer that many people miss it. You ask yourself the question that will give you the information you need. It's like doing research on the Internet. You have to find the right question for the search engine to get the answer you are looking for. You type in the question and here comes the answer. That's not the best analogy because the source of the answers is obviously different. You can see where the answers are coming from with the Internet. With intuition, you have no proof of where the answers are coming from. But it's similar, if you ask the right question, you're going to get the information you need."

"So do you always get an answer when you ask your intuition a question?"

"Actually, I usually *don't* get an answer right away. Sometimes I do. Sometimes I don't get an answer at all. When I don't get an answer, I figure there was something in the way. Maybe I'm not asking the right question. Maybe I need more time or to get more information. Or it's possible I may not be emotionally ready to hear the answer."

"I like all of those," she said.

"And the kind of question you are asking is important. If I am asking myself, 'What feels right for lunch?' the answer is important at the time but not of any great consequence in the grand scheme of things. If I am asking what I want to do with the rest of my life, that answer is going to require a much more complicated response. Some questions get answered right away. Some questions can seem like it takes forever. So it's definitely more of an art than a science."

"Do your intuitive answers produce the results you want?" she asked.

"Oh yeah. I kept a log for years just to prove this to myself. Whenever I made an intuitive choice, I kept track of how it worked out. It was very consistent. Sometimes the intuitive choice didn't work out right away, but it always worked out somehow and in ways I would have never imagined. That was the part that fascinated me the most and made me see the genius of our intuition. It clearly has access to information that our intellect does not have.

"Unfortunately, it seems like our intellect doesn't want to listen to our intuition. I guess it thinks intuition is dangerous because you can't see the path to the answer. There is no validation for how your intuition came up with its answer. And there is usually no proof that the intuitive answer will work. No validation and no proof make the cautious intellect nervous and cranky.

"Anyway, once I started to keep a log and reviewed it from time to time, it didn't take me long to see that my intuition was a whole lot smarter than my intellect. I can say without hesitation that the best things that have happened in my life have come from making intuitive choices and not from trying to figure things out with my intellect."

"I totally agree with everything you're saying," she said. "I find that most guys seem to get the concept of how intuition

51

works if you talk about sports. When you're playing any sport well, when you're 'in the zone,' what are you thinking about?"

"Nothing," I said. "It's an all-encompassing feeling, it's sheer awareness. I've played in ice hockey games where I was in that zone and able to do things I didn't know I could do!"

"Exactly. It's all awareness and intuitive instinct. Your intellect becomes a quiet, devoted assistant to your intuition. That's the way it's supposed to be and that's where we're headed, except the arena is much bigger than the ice rink," she said.

"Sounds like my kind of game."

"We can show you ways to hear your intuition at a whole new level."

A pretty Japanese face looked into our sanctuary. "You like dessert?"

"Dessert?" I looked at Sophia.

"You like green tea ice cream?"

"I do."

"Bring us one green tea ice cream and two spoons," she said to our impeccable hostess.

"So honey, I know you've had a rough day. You could have been killed by the car crash and then you had to deal with being in the hospital all afternoon. But here's the thing. I would love to say take a couple weeks and think about our offer to work for ASC and get back to us, but it doesn't work that way. We need you to make a decision—actually *choice* is a better word. A choice tends to be more intuitive, a decision tends to be more intellectual."

"What do I do with all my doubts and fears?" I asked.

"You bring them along with you. You don't let them stop you. There is always an unknown element in anything you do. The bigger the risk, the more fear you have to tangle with. The fear never goes away completely but you can learn to minimize its effects. And some fear will help you perform better by keeping you sharp.

"You have already been given your first assignment. You and I have spent enough time together for you to know if I'm a mental patient or not." She paused to give me a big smile. "So what do you think? Is everything I have told you some fantasy that I made up or can you tell there is truth here?"

"There is a big part of me that wants what you're saying to be true but there is a war going on inside my head. My instincts say that *you* believe that all of what you've told me is true, but my intellect is going nuts with how few people have any knowledge of your story. If you had some proof that what you're saying is true, that would help."

"Proof would make the decision much easier, but that's the rub. I'm not allowed to offer you any proof beyond what I have given. You have to make the decision to work with us without proof. That's the test of your intuitive instincts that we require," she said.

"If I were to offer to give you a back rub every day for a year, would you consider making an exception and give me just a little more proof?"

"You're adorable, and I love back rubs, but the answer's still no. Nice try, though. I like how you think."

"Are you willing to promise me that if I say yes, you're not going to drug me and sell me to an evil scientist as a test dummy for creating the ultimate weapon?"

She laughed. "I think *you* have watched too many spy movies."

"I have an active imagination."

"I like your imagination. We just need to get it focused on something besides talking pretty girls out of their panties."

"Am I that obvious?"

"The question is, what have you got to lose? And I just thought of a better way to pose the question. If your instincts say that my story is true, then I'm also giving you the choice of being a significant player in the most important game ever played. Or you can be a clueless observer in the stands. Which role do you want to play?"

"When you put it that way, it sounds like the bigger loss is not to go for it."

"Aha, so there *is* a brain to go with that darling face, overlooking a few stitches of course."

"Can I sleep on it?"

"I wish I could give you more time, honey, but I can't. If you don't know what you want to do by now, I can't take you. This is it. You have to choose tonight, in or out."

As I looked at her awaiting my response, I thought about how much I loved her looking at me. The truth was... something always felt right about Sophia.

"I'm in," I said. At that very moment, the earth actually did move as it sometimes does in L.A. Our conversation went on pause to see how long the gentle swaying movement would last and if anything dangerous would fall on us. It was short, about five seconds. It felt like a lot longer. You're always glad when the movement stops. I pray for it to stop the second it starts. It's a striking reminder of how much life is really out of our control.

"That was a little scary," she said. "Part of living on a fault line, I guess."

"I'm always glad when it stops," I said.

"Me too." She paused, took a big breath, and then moved on like nothing had happened. "One more time, I need to hear you make it official."

"I'm in."

"I'm glad." She glowed. "You and I can do some big things together, important things. There is nothing I would rather do than hang out and celebrate your choice to join the team, but I need a rain check. I have another meeting, and you've had quite a day. You need to go home and heal up. Let me walk you to the limo and Diego will take you home."

The ride home was short. I was exhausted. The cuts on my face and the general area of the back of my head were calling for a few Advil. As I got to the front door of my apartment, the door was ajar. There were no lights on inside. Did someone break in? Were they still there? I really didn't want to go back to the hospital tonight. I slowly opened the door, flipped on the light switch and couldn't believe my eyes. My things were all over the floor. The pictures were off the walls and smashed on the floor. The drawers in the kitchen had been taken out and dumped. The cushions in the couch and my big leather chair had been cut open and the stuffing was everywhere. The food in the refrigerator had been dumped onto the kitchen floor. It reeked of fish and onions. That felt mean.

It didn't feel like anyone was still there, but in order to feel safe I had to check every possible place someone could hide. What were they after? Anything of value I kept in a safety deposit box. I did a quick visual inventory. TV, stereo and camera were still there. My laptop was gone! Unbelievable! I hated the thought of going through the process of replacing my computer even with a recent backup. Whoever did this was just plain mean.

Was this related to working with Sophia? Should I call her and tell her what had happened? My instinct was to call her.

"Hi, sorry to bother you," I said. "My condo was tossed. It's totaled, just like my car."

"Are you okay?"

"Yeah, they were gone before I got here."

"Anything missing?"

"My laptop."

"Call the police. Your insurance company will respond better with a police report. I will send a bodyguard over right away to watch your place tonight."

"Really, you think that's necessary?"

"Absolutely. You need to get some sleep tonight. The police report is going to take a while. You will sleep better if someone is there. Sleep in tomorrow. I will meet you at your place mid-morning. The code name for the bodyguard will be the restaurant where we first met. He will text you the code name, his license plate number and then you will have his cell number on your phone if you need him. He will park where he can see your place."

"I don't believe this," I said.

"I have to go. Hang in there."

6. Fire the Judge...

"Hi-ee. Can I come in?" said Sophia through my screen door.

"Yes, please come in. I was just thinking about you," I said.

"I know, I could feel that high-powered brain of yours consuming massive quantities of energy a block away."

"Is that normal?"

"For you it is, but not to worry, mental energy is something we have in abundant supply."

"Good, that makes me feel better. I would hate to be unknowingly using up all the brain energy and making everyone else around me dumb and slow." I said that as a joke and then wondered if that was actually possible.

"Don't worry, sugar. You can't slow me down if you tried. You just keep being your sweet self and don't give it another thought... I like your place and you're so close to the beach."

I liked to work at my large oak dining room table, which was one of the few things that had not been scratched, cut or destroyed in last night's raid. I could sit at my big table and look out through a large picture window with a view of the street and the row of beach houses that were between me and the ocean. I had an upstairs apartment in a converted mansion that was built in the 1940s. I actually had a view of the ocean from my balcony. The building had seen its better days, but the trees were huge and the grounds well maintained. And it was relatively quiet most of the time aside from a little traffic noise.

I had several clients in various stages of buying financial products from me and many prospects to get back to. Sophia had said we could use my current sales projects to start my training. I had no idea what she had planned, but that was why we were meeting at my apartment.

"Yes, it's small, but I like it here. Unfortunately, things are not as nice as they were yesterday," I said.

"I'm sorry your place got tossed. It doesn't look too bad."

"I got up early this morning and did my best. You have no idea how much stuff you have until somebody dumps it all in the middle of the room. I lost some valuable art and my furniture is all cut up, as you can see. I threw a lot in the trash."

"How did it go with the police?"

"Boring and uneventful, an hour's worth of paperwork."

"Have you talked to the insurance agent?"

"Yes, they're going to cover most of my stuff, but you know how that goes. Some things are not replaceable, and I can't get the full value on the art I lost, and it takes time to go through the process of replacing everything. I'm angry and I feel violated. I'd like to find the SOB that did this and do a number on him and his place. Plastic explosives come to mind."

"Your anger is totally justified. This kind of thing is a major invasion of privacy and incredibly disruptive. But I need you to listen to me and trust me. There are menacing types who don't like us and try their best to make our lives more difficult. I can't tell you any more than that right now. What I need you to hear is that the importance of this job is worth having to occasionally deal with the bad guys. There are those who don't want change and will do anything to stop it. You are a new guy, and they like to see if they can rattle the rookies. So can you include this inconvenience as part of the job and trust me that there will be ways to more than make up for it?" she said.

"Nothing like this has ever happened to me before. I was expecting to be one of the lucky ones and not have negative things happen to me. I realize now that was a stupid expectation."

"This is a test of your vision. You have to be able to maintain a positive vision of yourself and the mission, no matter what happens. If you allow any negativity to linger or fail to find value in what you're being taught, you become the weak link in the chain."

"I don't want to be the weak link."

"I know you don't, and you're being given an important lesson right now. Your best response is to look for the lesson and become stronger not weaker. If you become weaker, the bad guys win."

"Do you know what the lesson is?" I asked.

"I just told you part of it."

"Can you give me a hint? My mind is a fog."

"It's about not letting negative things get you down."

"Has your place ever been tossed?"

"Yes. You do what you have to do and move on. We don't have the luxury of slowing down to feel bad. So. you ready to go to work? Is the coffee on?" She was forcing a smile. "Tell me about your life insurance thing." She was finding her spot at my dining room table.

"Just like that? We're not going to talk anymore about how I feel that my place was turned into a trash heap? I'm angry and frustrated."

"Honey, the important thing is that you're okay. Yes, it's a hassle, but you're going to get new stuff. We don't have the time or the luxury to feel sorry for ourselves when the bad guys get in the way. It won't be the last time. So, yes, just like that, we need to move on." There was conviction in her tone.

She expected me to move on. To my amazement, I let go of my anger and moved on.

"And if you find that you still need to talk to someone about what happened to release it, make an appointment with Angela. That's her job and she's a skilled counselor. Can you be with *me* now and get some work done?"

"Okay. This is all new to me, but I get what you're saying."

"Good. So how do you help people with their life insurance?" she said.

"Well, I help them maximize what they're doing with their conservative money."

"How do you do that?"

"They taught me to ask if they would like to save some money on their life insurance. I say that people are living longer and that has substantially lowered the premiums. Then I ask if they would like to find out how much I could save them."

"Does that work?"

"It works okay. I get some appointments. Once I get to know people a little, they like me, and I make some sales. Not as many as I would like to make. When I see the sales numbers of the more successful advisors in our office, I'm always dumbfounded. I don't know how they write so much business."

"I know exactly how they do it," she said. "I got recruited from a sales job to work on the LightSpace Project. I was one of the most successful salespeople in the history of the company. I set a bunch of records and got to go on orgasmic trips to some of the most exotic places you could ever imagine. But we have to save the show-and-tell for later. We have too much to do right now. The point I wanted to make was that my products were a little different, but the principles for making sales *and making big sales* are the same."

"Will you teach me how to make big sales, Obi-wan? You are my only hope." I was going for a smile, and I wanted her help. I got both.

"Of course. It's not something you see right away, but the skills required to be a master salesperson are right in line with those required to make the jump to lightspace. That's how I got to be one of the project leaders. My selling and communication skills made me as good as anybody at promoting lightspace.

"Most people think that sales is about talking you into buying things. To me it was always more about helping others get exactly what they want. Help people get what they want and most of them will buy. Some will buy big!"

"I am soft clay awaiting the skilled touch of the master sculptor."

"Let's hope you turn out better than the ashtray I made for my daddy when I was seven!"

"I'll do whatever you tell me to do," I said.

"That *is* one of your more endearing qualities."

"What do we do next?"

"Bathroom break. Your tasty Grand Marnier coffee went right through me."

"End of the hall on your left," I said. "Try to ignore the mess." I was embarrassed that the first time she saw my place, it was in shambles.

"Don't give it another thought. It'll all be fixed up before you know it."

I was eager to get Sophia's input. No matter what I did, I wanted to be a master at selling myself, my ideas and whatever projects I was involved in. I had been told I was good at sales and promotion. Most of the people I talked to would buy something from me, but I always struggled with finding enough of the right potential clients to talk to, which held me back.

Sophia walked back into the room. "First, let's change your phone script. It's okay, but it doesn't have much pulling power. You need to talk about the benefits for the potential client. You want to be hard to say no to."

"You have that part down," I said. "I knew I'd have a hard time saying no to you the first time I saw you!"

"Luke, you say the nicest things." Her tone and her gaze were flirty and inviting. She was, after all, in my apartment. I had imagined numerous times how easy it would be for us to get hot and sweaty. But then she got back to business.

"Let's give the folks some inspired reasons to get together with you. You can do a lot more than just save them money. You can help them plan their financial futures, avoid costly mistakes and realize their dreams!"

"That's all true. Should I say that on the phone?"

"That might be a little much for your opener. How about you call your prospect and do whatever opening you want, then say, 'John, I'm on a major campaign to help everyone I know and care about maximize what they're doing with their conservative money, and you're on my list!

'What I typically do is spend an hour with you. I'll teach you as much as I can in that hour. I'll answer your questions. We will talk about anything else that's important to you.

'I don't charge for this, and there's nothing to buy. This is a free service. Typically, I can make or save you thousands of dollars, sometimes tens of thousands of dollars, just from this single meeting. Does that sound like that might be helpful to you?'"

"Sold! I love it," I said. "When can we get together?"

"What do you like about it?" she asked.

"Well, obviously I'm calling people I know or have met, if I know and care about them. I like saying that because I *do* care about them. I like the idea that you are going to teach me things I need to know and answer my questions. I don't need any money to do this, so this is a free service and you are going to make or save me some money on top of that. I've got everything to gain and nothing to lose."

"Exactly. Do you hear the difference?"

"I can't wait to try it."

"How about right now?" she said. "Do you have some acquaintances we can call to give this a test drive?"

"Sure, but I'd like to practice this a little first. I don't want to blow it and sound like a beginner."

"Come on, a pickup artist like you can rattle that language off in your sleep!"

"Yeah, but there is a little more involved here. I really want to do this right."

"So you're fearless when it comes to talking women into the bedroom, but when it comes to talking to a potential client you're not so daring?"

"Pull the dagger out of my gut. You're not supposed to know that!"

"Too late. So what are you afraid of?"

"What is this, truth or dare?" I said.

"No, this is truth or consequences. Do you want to keep living with the fear or do you want to get rid of it?"

"I want to get rid of it," I said. Admitting a weakness to the woman I so wanted to impress was hard.

"Do you trust me? What if I told you I was so scared, I used to stare at the phone for hours before I could pick it up to make one call."

"You?" I said in disbelief.

"*The one and only.*"

"How did you overcome your fear?"

"That's where we're headed, but I need you to tell me you want to do this first. If you and I are going to carry a couch up a flight of stairs, I'm not going to get very far if you don't carry your end."

"No, I guess not."

"So are you ready to jump off the cliff with me and learn to fly on the way down or would you rather do this tomorrow?"

"Is tomorrow an option?" I said.

"You're a funny fella, and you know it's not. For some, tomorrow is an option, but for you and who I need you to be, it's not. There are too many dear souls already counting on you that you haven't even met yet. I need you fearless across the board."

"You've pulled my pants down. I feel totally exposed. What happens now?"

"Raise your right hand. No, pull up your pants first and then raise your right hand." She paused to see how I would respond.

"I can get my pants on and off with no hands."

"Let's definitely save that for later. Let's stick with raise your right hand and repeat after me..."

"I, Luke Lamaire, do hereby solemnly swear..."

"I, Luke Lamaire, do hereby solemnly swear..."

"...to do whatever it takes to overcome my fears with Sophia's expert help."

"...to do whatever it takes to overcome my fears with Sophia's expert help."

"There now, doesn't that feel better?"

"You mean now that I've been totally humiliated in front of my rock star boss, who I'm desperately trying to impress?"

"I appreciate the thought, doll, but that kind of thinking will get in the way of you and me being at our best. The last thing I want you thinking about is what I think about you. I want you trusting those great instincts of yours knowing I have your back, no matter what. And that I'm thinking good thoughts about you, pants up or pants down. That's what I call horsepower!"

"Okay. I got it. That's what I want, too. I want to play full out with you and hold nothing back."

"That's the stud I want on my ranch!"

"I really could use a shot of Herradura right now," I said.

"Yeah, I know. Thank Party Guy and Scared Guy for sharing, and let's wake up the team of Committed Guy, Resourceful Guy and Gutsy Guy and keep going, shall we? I'd like to have a major breakthrough before lunch."

I yawned. "Do you ever get tired? I feel exhausted."

She ignored me. "First, I want you to imagine getting ready to call someone you know. What are your concerns?"

"They might say no."

"What else are you afraid might happen?"

"I would feel bad because I put my friend on the spot and made him feel uncomfortable. *I* would feel uncomfortable. I was trained to think that if I don't get an appointment then I have failed, so I'd feel bad about that."

"What else?"

"What else!? Isn't that enough?"

"How does it make you feel when you think about having a friend say no to you on the phone?" she asked.

"Embarrassed. Sleazy. Disappointed in myself. I feel like a loser. I feel like a failure. I wonder what I'm doing wrong. Others with far less intelligence seem to do this easily. I wonder whether I'm in the right job? I feel like I want to go to the Beach Bar, pour myself a cold one and forget about all this madness."

"Tell you what... You give me 100 percent of that super-computer in your head and a little of that big heart of yours and I will take you to the Beach Bar myself and have a cold one with you. Deal?"

"Deal. I could use something to look forward to."

"Okay, play along with me. Let's pretend you're at the beach and you see a hot babe that's making your heart beat a little faster than normal. What do you do?"

"That would depend on a number of things. I would create an excuse to talk to her. I would say something to get a conversation started."

"Would you try to say something clever?"

"Probably not. Being clever puts pressure on her to be clever back. Most women don't like that kind of pressure. You, on the other hand, have no problem in that department!"

"You consider me a worthy adversary?"

"No question about that!"

"You're right. I've heard every line you can imagine," she said. "I tend to think the guys who aren't trying so hard have more confidence. If a guy has the right frame of mind, I don't need much more than a sexy 'hello' to get my juices flowing. Am I easy or what?"

"*Easy* isn't the word that comes to mind."

"I think I got us a little off track here," she said. "Let's get back to our babe at the beach."

"Ideally I would look for a way to get her to smile. If I can't find that, almost anything will work. Even something as overused as the weather works. The most important thing is to say something, like you just confirmed. If it's someone you're going to enjoy being with, she's going to respond to anything you say that's sincere. Then I listen for what comes to me as I'm with her. That's the intuitive part."

"I know a lot of guys who would feel a bit uneasy with your intuitive approach," she said.

"Yeah, I guess I don't think about it much, I just do it. I'm not sure how I learned to do it."

"I can tell you one thing you're not doing that makes you really good at starting conversations with women."

"What's that?"

"You don't judge yourself or what you're saying. You don't panic. You're not trying to do it right. You just listen for what to say—it comes to you and then you say it. The same way you described playing hockey and singing on stage. Sheer awareness."

"I guess that's right," I said.

"If you want to be as good at sales as you are at talking to women, you have to learn to stop negatively judging what you're saying. When you allow negative judgment, you hear commands in your head. 'Do this, don't do that! This is right, that's wrong. Or, don't do it that way, stupid!' It's a big mess.

"The internal commands are followed by negative feelings like frustration, fear, doubt, worry, or some horrible combination. There are so many distractions and so much

66

negative feeling going on, you're an emotional disaster, which makes you a conversational Neanderthal. And most important, guess what you can't hear?"

"What?" I said. I wanted to scream.

"Your intuitive voice! That genius part of you that knows what to say in any situation. That guy on stage who knows exactly how to sing the song to move the audience. The part of you that can hang out in the middle of a crisis and wait for just the right time to take action."

"I get it. So how do I stop judging? That seems impossible."

"I think you need to move. We need both sides of that large brain of yours functioning. Walk down to the ocean and back at a medium pace while I make a couple of calls. When you get back, we will do a *warm-up*. You will be able to make calls more easily than ever before, I promise."

"All right, I hope you're right. I'll take a short walk."

"Get out of your head and into your body," she said. "Feel yourself breathing. Do a few stretches. Focus on what it feels like to just walk."

"I've got a few dance moves I do when I walk to make it more creative."

"Now you're talking. Go find your rhythm."

7. Rolling the Dice...

As I approached my apartment after an energetic fifteen-minute walk with some stretching, Sophia was holding the door open for me.

"How do you feel now?" she said.

"I still like hanging out with you more than I enjoy making sales calls."

"It's your lucky day, you get to do both," she said.

"I wish I had as much confidence in me as you do."

"Don't worry, you don't need confidence, you need guts. And you have the guts of a burglar. You let your worries keep you from making calls, and I have to show you how to stop that. Which, if I understand correctly, is something you want to learn how to do."

"You are great, you are wise," I said with a bow.

"That's good. You keep that sense of humor around when you're making calls and you'll have no trouble at all. Who was the worrier when you were growing up?"

"My mother. She thought her job in life was to worry about her children, and everything else for that matter."

"A lot of people think that worrying helps somehow," she said. "It doesn't! Worrying is a form of negative thinking that

68

is our biggest enemy in the fight for lightspace. Under pressure, most people create a negative vision of what *could* happen. Then they worry about the negative vision they created. That is not a resourceful state for living your life."

"So it's a war against negativity," I said.

"That's the battle. There are people who think it's positive to worry about all the things that *could* go wrong and keep track of what they did wrong so they don't do it again. But if you're focused on the negative, guess what you create more of?"

"The negative."

"If you say to yourself, 'Don't be afraid of the phone,' what does your mind have to do first?"

"Think about being afraid of the phone."

"Right. Then what's step two?"

"Try not to be afraid of the phone."

"It doesn't work. The message to your brain is *be afraid of the phone*," she said.

"So how do we kill off the *fear of the phone monster* once and for all?"

"We have to get the right guys in your head at the front of the bus."

"Which guys do you want?" I asked.

"Gutsy Guy, Intuitive Guy, Resourceful Guy and Outgoing Guy for sure."

"Who do you want me to move to the back?"

"Scared Guy, Analytical Guy, Worried Guy and Skeptical Guy. Let's move them to the back of the bus and let them watch movies about the end of the world."

I chuckled at the irony. "I feel better already."

"That's a good sign. All right, I have a present for you. Close your eyes and give me your hand."

"That reminds me of a couple jokes."

"Stay with me now. No time to travel back to the fraternity house. Close your eyes." She put something square with sharp edges in my hand and then closed my hand. There were two of them. "Keep your eyes closed for a minute. I'm not done with this part yet."

"I think I can guess what they are!" I sounded like a little kid.

"Shhh! Let me finish my ceremony." She gently placed both of her hands around my hand. "These are special dice that will always remind you that *if you keep rolling the dice, you will roll a winner*. The only way you can lose is to stop rolling the dice. I want you to feel my love in these dice and my love for you as a partner in the most important mission in history."

"Thanks. That means a lot."

The energy this beauty could generate would light up a small city. Combine that with her pure love and you were ready to move mountains.

"Open your eyes," she said.

There were two large crystal-clear red dice with white dots. The casino name was stamped in a circle around each snake eye.

"I have given you two registered dice from the Hard Rock Casino in Las Vegas. They have actually been rolled on the roulette tables there at least once. More important is for you to be aware of the energy I have given them."

"I'll remember."

"Okay, Romeo, let's do a warm-up for getting you on the phone. Here's how it works. I say a reason not to make a call. Then you repeat the reason out loud after me and then roll your dice. Sevens, elevens and doubles are appointments. Anything else is a call that didn't go anywhere. You roll ten times. Write down how many appointments you get. Got it?"

"Let's do it," I said.

"Number one. Repeat after me: 'I don't feel like prospecting today.' Then roll the dice."

"Okay. 'I don't feel like prospecting today.' Seven! Got my first appointment."

"Did anyone ever call you *dumb luck*?" she said. "Number two: 'It never seems like the right time to call.'"

"'It never seems like the right time to call.' Five. No appointment, darn."

"Number three: 'This person is probably already working with a financial advisor.'"

"'This person is probably already working with a financial advisor.' Doubles, two threes, appointment!"

"That's good, two out of three," she said. "Number four: 'I'm not sure what to say to this person.'"

"'I'm not sure what to say to this person.' Nine. Boo..."

"Number five: 'I can make these calls tomorrow.'"

"'I can make these calls tomorrow.' Eleven, appointment!"

"You know the most significant thing about tomorrow?" she asked.

"What's that?"

"Tomorrow never comes. Number six: 'I don't have time to prospect.'"

"'I don't have time to prospect.' A three plus one is four. Shoot!"

"Now let me ask you an important question," she said. "Do the dice care what you are thinking before you roll them?"

"No."

"Does what you are thinking have any effect on the dice?"

"Probably not. No."

"Precisely. The dice do their own thing regardless of what you are thinking. Number seven: 'Prospecting takes too much time.'"

"'Prospecting takes too much time.' Three plus five is eight. Foiled again!"

"Number eight: Fill in the blank, 'I would rather be...'"

"'I would rather be saving the world with Sophia.' Eleven, appointment!"

"I like your answer," she said. "Number nine: A special one for you innovators and rebels, 'There has to be an easier way!'"

71

"'There has to be an easier way!' I like that one," I said. "Six and four. Another dog."

"And last, number ten: For the experienced advisor like yourself, 'I've paid my dues. I shouldn't have to make these calls!'"

"'I've paid my dues. I shouldn't have to make these calls!' Snake eyes! All right!"

"Count up your appointments," she said.

"Five out of ten."

"How do you feel about that?"

"If I can get five out of ten appointments, they'll be talking about me around the water cooler!"

"How many appointments you got isn't what's important, however. Let me ask you a couple more questions to make my point. Can you roll the dice correctly?" she asked.

"No. You might think you can, but not really."

"Can you control the dice?"

"No. Not really."

"Does it matter what you think of before you roll the dice?"

"No."

"Can you get an appointment if you don't roll?"

"No."

"So what conclusion would you make from this exercise?" she asked.

"The most important thing is to roll the dice. *If you don't roll, there is no possibility for success.*"

"Your hockey brother Wayne Gretzky said something like 'You miss 100 percent of the shots you don't take.'"

"He did say that. I'm impressed."

"Do you know how these people are going to respond before you make the call?"

"No idea," I said.

"So do you hear what you're saying? You have no idea how people are going to respond until you make the call! So where do your fears, doubts, worries and other concerns come from?"

"Past experience?" Seemed like the right answer to me.

"Correct! Do they have anything at all to do with the call you are about to make?"

"No. It's a totally new call."

"That's the opening or window where you can make calls with no resistance. Do you get it? Can you see it? Can you feel it?"

"Yeah, the window is making calls without remembering any past experience to make you afraid or anxious," I said.

"That's it. If you had amnesia and couldn't remember any of your past prospecting calls, would you have any call reluctance?"

"No."

"No is right. You would have no reference point to make you worried or fearful or negative in any way. What do you suppose is next?"

"To make calls?" I said tentatively.

"Good answer. We also need to keep you in good shape by controlling the quality of your calls. Have you ever had calls not go very well?" she asked.

"Sure."

"How did that make you feel?"

"Lousy."

"What went wrong or what didn't work?" she asked.

"It's usually because the other guy gives you a hard time."

"So not very friendly."

"Not at all."

"How do the calls go if the other person is friendly?" she said.

"Usually pretty good. I may not get an appointment but it's a decent experience."

"So here's rule #3. Don't talk to anyone who's giving you a hard time or who's in a lousy mood."

"How do I do that?"

"It's easy. You just push any three numbers." She pressed three numbers on the phone. "Then hang up. They think something went wrong with the phone when they hear the three beep tones. That gives you a way out. They're glad to be off the phone and they won't call back."

"So if I don't like what's happening on the call, I push three buttons and bail."

"That's rule #3. Stay in a good mood. Enjoy making calls. Have fun making calls. If you get an attitude on the other end, you bail. You don't let civilians with a bad attitude bring your vibration down."

"I feel like a moron for asking, but what's Rule #1 and #2?"

"Rule #1 is: *You can't make an appointment without rolling the dice!* Rule #2 is: *Isolate yourself from your past and you have no fear.*"

"I knew that," I said. Having fun with Sophia made this discussion tolerable. I was trying to ignore the fact that I could be making a total fool of myself in front of her at any moment.

"Do you have your script and some prospects to call?" she asked.

"I do."

"What are you feeling?"

"Nervous, excited. A little concerned that the guy on the other end might yell at me and tell me to go to hell. Other than that, I'm having a great time."

"Let's do this. Dial your first number."

I dialed the phone. She kissed me on the cheek and whispered, "Remember, it doesn't matter what happens. You can't lose with me."

"Hello, John. Luke Lamaire. How are you?"

"Hey Luke, how are you? I haven't talked to you in a long time. What's up?"

"John, you know I've been in the financial services business for a number of years. Well, I have learned a lot about how to help people maximize what they are doing with their conservative money, and I wanted to tell you more about what I'm doing.

"I spend an hour with people. I will teach you as much as I can in that hour about what smart folks are doing with their money. I'll answer your questions. I don't charge for this. There's nothing to buy. Typically, I can make or save you thousands, sometimes tens of thousands of dollars, just from this single meeting.

"Does that sound like that might be helpful to you?"

"Well, I'm not sure. I have an advisor I work with, and I think he's pretty good."

"John, most people today have one or more advisors. Here's what I can do. I will give you the information, and if you like, you can share it with your advisor. I am mainly on an educational campaign at this point. Let me buy you a cup of coffee and give you some ideas that will make you money. What do you say to that?"

"Well, I guess that wouldn't hurt anything. Sure, why not."

I finished up the call with John and set the appointment for next week.

"How'd I do, coach?"

"Nice job. I liked everything about that call. I especially liked how you handled his response that he already had an advisor. Well done. So that didn't appear to be particularly life-threatening for you to make that call. Was it?" she said teasingly.

"That was an easy one. I know him from hockey. Actually, I am realizing I'm fine once I get someone on the phone. My problem is getting myself to make the calls."

"I understand. We will work on that. We can cure the resistance you have by changing how you think. Now pick someone you don't know very well or not at all."

"I have a lot of those."

"Before you dial, a question: What are you feeling right now?"

"The usual. I'm not sure this will work. I don't want to get yelled at. I don't want to hear no. I don't want to be rejected. I have a general feeling of anxiety."

"What you're feeling is normal. We have to refocus. Does it matter what happens on any one call?" she asked.

"No."

"Do you have any control over what happens on any one call?"

"No, not really."

"Have a good time. It doesn't matter what happens. It's *all* out of your control. Offer a lot. Listen for interest. If it's not happening after a couple of tries, move on."

"Let's smile and dial!" I said. The line was ringing. "Somebody told me this guy was looking for an advisor but didn't want me to use their name."

"Hello!" blasted a gruff voice.

"Hello, this is Luke Lamaire. Is Dick there?"

"Whadda-ya-want?" he barked.

I sensed Sophia trying to get my attention. I looked at her, and she was holding up three fingers. So I pushed three buttons on the phone and hung up.

"How did that feel?"

"That felt great! I had a horrible feeling in my stomach when that guy answered the phone. What a jerk. It felt really good to be able to just dump him and hang up the phone."

"Right on!" she said, raising her fist in the air. "*Dump that dude with the bad atti-tude!* You don't need to interact with that horrible energy."

"You've been a huge help today."

"My pleasure. You're fun to work with. You learn fast, and your heart's in the right place once we get you past your resistance. Those qualities are hard to teach. And, you got to see how to shift to a bigger perspective to overcome fears, doubts, worry, anxiety, etc. We will make you a master at that process and a wizard at teaching it to others."

"I like the sound of that. What's next, boss?"

"I think it's time you meet some of your peers. Are you free tonight?"

"I'll arrange it."

"Candy will contact you with details. I need to run." She raised her hand toward me. It looked like a high five, except she had her fingers spread apart.

I laced my fingers between hers and gently closed my hand. I wanted to pull her to me and kiss her but somehow managed to restrain myself.

"We did good today," she said.

"You helped me a lot. Thank you."

8. Sounds Like a Party...

Candy texted me and said to be at the office at 7 p.m. Attire was casual. I wasn't sure what casual attire meant with this crowd. In L.A., some partygoers like to dress up, and some like to put their creativity into seeing how uniquely casual they can look. It's not uncommon to see tuxedos and evening gowns mixed with tattered jeans and a neon tank top. I figured casual attire meant wear whatever you want. A blazer, slacks and golf shirt defined comfort for me.

As I walked in the front door of the office, Candy was patiently explaining something to an older woman. I waited for her to make eye contact and then she motioned for me to head down the hall.

I walked toward the voices that sounded more like a party. I heard a woman's laugh that I would now recognize anywhere. I knew I was headed in the right direction.

I knocked as I slowly opened the door and peeked in. "Hello, hello... Is everyone decent?"

The first face I saw was a new one—a slender, attractive female about thirty with electric red hair neatly pulled back. She wore a lacy white blouse, tattered blue jeans and high, rust-colored leather boots, a sultry pirate. I liked the look. And she had a wonderful smile.

"Hi, I'm Renee," she said, extending her hand to shake. "And you are?"

"Luke. I'm the new guy."

"Luke, of course, welcome. Sophia has been telling us all about you. Everyone's looking forward to meeting you. Come right in. Stay right here for a second, and I'll get Sophia."

"Thank you."

I didn't know what to expect, but I was thinking I would be meeting a handful of people. This had the feel of a serious party that had been going on for a while with upwards of two hundred people. Hey, I worked in a busy nightclub, this felt like home to me.

"Luke…"

I heard my new favorite voice call my name. I turned and was rewarded with a vision of poise and grace.

"Hey, you're right on time," Sophia said. "The meeting will start in a few minutes." She gently grabbed my arm and pulled me into the crowd behind her. She was radiant. Every few steps she would get a smile or a nod or a "Hi, Sophia!" as we moved to the front of the crowded room.

We were in the ballroom. There was a large stage platform about a foot and a half high with a couple of large blackboards toward the back that had been used and erased a few times. Antique bronze lamps with a single large white globe hung from the high ceiling surrounding an elaborate crystal chandelier in the middle of the room. There were stacks of chairs along the outside walls. The hardwood floor added an elegance and simplicity of a time long past. The energy in the room was charged, the mood was happy and familiar like everyone had done this before. This was not a shy group. It was loud with frequent bursts of laughter coming from different directions. A twenty-something gent with an athletic build in a dark business suit and no tie carried a director's chair, a music stand and a lapel microphone to the middle of the stage. He looked at Sophia. "You ready?"

"Born ready," she said.

He set up the chair with the music stand to the side and gave Sophia the microphone.

Her voice boomed over the crowd noise. "Good evening, everyone! In preparation for the next part of our meeting tonight, let's have the strong guys and gals unstack the chairs so you all have a place to sit. Leave a nice open space down the middle to keep the fire department happy."

I was fascinated to watch the room transform. We were about to get down to business with our gorgeous, fearless leader taking center stage. I was as impressed as ever.

This was a new side of Sophia that gave the program all the more credibility. Much of the crowd looked like they had come from work either dressed up or business casual, and there were just as many creatively dressed types that could have come from anywhere, about half men and half women and all ages and nationalities, which was normal in L.A. White people are actually a minority in Los Angeles County, which I always found interesting compared to growing up in a totally Caucasian small town in the Midwest. I couldn't tell their jobs or their ranks in the grand scheme of things, but there was no question they all respected Sophia.

"Okay, let's get started. A couple of quick announcements. Janet Jones got the lead in the new movie with Shia Labeouf. Way to go, Janet!"

There was tremendous applause with equal amounts of hoot and holler and a few whistles for the pretty Miss Jones.

"Also, as most of you know, on the political front, Jason Gardner was re-elected as state senator last week. Congratulations, Jason."

Again major applause with a little more decorum for the senator.

"If there are any other announcements or member acknowledgments, be sure to let Candy know so it gets on the agenda.

"Getting to our business for this evening, first I want to welcome the new recruits who are here for the first time tonight. And one of you is someone I recruited myself. As you know, I need skilled enrollers to get as many new candidates into our program as possible this year, and I found the perfect guy! Luke, can you come up and say hello, and tell us a little about yourself?"

As I walked toward the end of the stage where the microphone was, I was surprised at how calm I felt. It was like I was being helped somehow.

"Hi, everyone. I'm Luke Lamaire. This all happened kind of fast. One minute I am trying to get the attention of a beautiful woman, and the next thing you know I have a new job, a new career, really." I could tell by their smiles they knew what I was talking about.

"And I'm excited. I'm excited to be part of such a resourceful group of people with such an important mission. I've lived here in Southern California most of my adult life. I've been involved in the nightclub business for many years and do some sales work during the daylight hours. Somehow, my skills seem to fit what Sophia is looking for, so here I am, ready to do my part. I look forward to working with you all."

I expected some applause when I finished. What I had not anticipated were the warmth and appreciation I got from this big room of strangers. That's a lot to feel from some applause, but it was very clear.

"Thanks, Luke. He is being modest about his skills. We are counting on Luke not only to be one of our top recruiters within a relatively short amount of time but also to be one of our top trainers. He is going to be a very busy man, so be sure to help him in any way you can.

"We have a lot of ground to cover tonight, so let's break into our groups now so you can do your regular business. You have thirty minutes to get as much done as you can. Be your brilliant, resourceful selves, and we will get back together at 8:10."

There was instant pandemonium as more than two hundred beings turned their chairs into small circles with everyone talking at the same time. Sophia gestured that she wanted to speak to me and then told me she needed a few minutes to deal with the group who had swarmed her on the stage. There was a lot going on. I had no idea as to the details, but their passion and enthusiasm were apparent. That was verifying for me to witness and exhilarating because I was going to get to be part of all this energy.

Fifteen minutes of listening to Sophia handle all kinds of logistical details had passed. Finally, even with a few folks still waiting to speak with her, she excused herself and said they were first when she came back. She walked in my direction and signaled me to follow her. We headed back to her office. She closed the door behind us.

"Sit down. I need a few minutes to chill," she said.

"Do you want me to find something to do?"

"No, stay here. I want you here. I just need to bring my energy level down a few notches. Interacting with this group is like plugging myself into an electric socket. You don't have the same effect on me—which is a good thing."

"I won't try to figure out what that means."

"You don't need to."

She looked into my eyes for about ten seconds. It felt like a long time. I was wondering what she was thinking. I was hoping it was good.

"So what did you think of this group?" she asked.

"I felt very welcome and accepted. That was an amazing feeling all by itself, to feel that accepted by a big group of people who don't know me."

"We're all kindred spirits. We all have a lot in common even though we haven't known each other very long in this reality. We have known each other before, but we don't need to get into that right now."

"I want to learn more about that when the time is right."

"Actually, the details of what happened in the past are not important. What *is* important is the feeling we have now for each other because of what happened in the past. If you subconsciously or intuitively feel good about someone, you are going to trust them a lot quicker and work as a team better than when you don't have that history together. We need every advantage we can get."

"So you have knowledge of this background when you recruit?"

"Yes and no. It kind of happens anyway because of rapport and chemistry. Probably more important from a recruiting standpoint is what kind of a path the person is on now. What are they here to learn this time? What have they completed in the past? When you find a person whose life mission fits our job description, and they have either developed the skills or have started to develop the skills we need, we have a star candidate."

"Did you have that kind of information about me?"

"Sure we did. Your ability to mix drinks and pick up beautiful women were not our main criteria. Although I'm not saying those skills won't come in handy." She laughed.

Hearing her laugh and seeing her smile right then moved me in a way that was distantly familiar. It reminded me of the total devotion the men in Joan of Arc's army had for her in a movie I'd seen. Those men were so committed to her, they would have gladly given their lives if that was required. You would be considered crazy to feel that way about anyone in today's society.

"I can tell people believe in you," I said. "I have my own sense of you, but it was good to experience how others feel about you firsthand. What is happening to me seems like a dream. To see that all these bright souls get who you are makes this all very real."

"They have to like me. I'm their CEO."

"What I saw was way more than being nice to the boss."

"So give me your perception of this crowd. What's the vibe you get?"

"You can feel when people are special. They have a personal presence, a depth to their being, an openness and you feel love trickling through."

"Good answer, honey." She stood up from the chair. "I'm revived. I like what happens to me when I spend time with you. I'm ready to get back in the fray. This meeting will go late. Stay as long as you want and don't hesitate to take off and do personal stuff. You'll have lots of time to get to know this crowd."

I got up and casually saluted goodbye as she dialed her phone. I got a quick smile on top of her many thoughts. I really wanted a hug, but that felt a little mushy for her mood. It was time for me to get out of the way and let her conquer the world, literally.

I decided to rejoin the group and meet a few more aspirants. Sophia's introduction of me advanced me to semi-celebrity status. The number of people who went out of their way to introduce themselves and make me feel at home made a lasting impression. It was a compelling confirmation that my instincts about Sophia were right-on.

I took Sophia's advice and headed out early. I was about to walk out the front door when I saw Candy doing something at the reception area.

"Candy, you should be back there partying with the troops."

"Yeah, I know, but duty calls. There is always a lot to do when this tribe shows up."

"I'll bet. Well, I'm headed home. See you tomorrow."

"Luke, I have a quick question."

"Sure." I walked over to where she was standing by the long counter. There was no one else around.

"You remember our little secret from the other day?"

"Of course. It's still our secret."

"I was wondering if you might consider sharing another little secret with me." She was adept at being shy and endearing.

"I guess, sure, what is it?"

"I don't know how else to tell you this other than just to say it."

"Go for it," I said.

"I get really horny, and I think you're hot. I'm sure you noticed I wear short skirts and knee socks, and part of my secret is that I also don't wear a bra or panties. I was wondering if I could interest you in an occasional quickie when we're alone in the office or wherever we might be. Nothing complicated, just a little passion to take the edge off. You know what I mean?"

"Candy, I don't know what to say. I think you're hot. But I'm not sure—" Before I could finish my sentence, she reached between my legs and slowly brushed her hand up the front of my pants. I was speechless and at immediate attention. Then she stuck her hand in my shirt to touch my bare stomach. Her eyes were glued to mine. I was frozen in her spell.

"Unfortunately," she said, barely touching her tongue to my ear, "I have an errand to run, and it's dark out there. Could you walk me to my car?"

The next word out of my mouth was, "Sure."

Candy was on a mission once we got in the backseat of her Grand Cherokee and pushed up her skirt. I let her take charge and tell me what she wanted. You could say I just went along for the ride, and what a ride it was. *Passionate* and *aerobic* are words that come to mind. And I'm happy to report that the rest of her body was just as firm and toned as those Olympic legs.

True to her word, Candy kept it short and sweet and sent me on my way with a smile on her face that said she was most pleased.

When I got home, I texted my temp bodyguard to make sure there had been no suspicious activity. He gave me the all-clear. It really did help me sleep to have someone keeping an eye on my place. I knew it wasn't likely that the intruders would be back anytime soon. But still, it was a whole new reality for me that my private property wasn't private anymore. I then decided I would sleep better if I reminisced my erotic twirl with Candy rather than give the bad guys another thought.

9. The Club...

My day was spent attending to as many logistical items as I could tolerate. I was organized and liked things a certain way. It was a huge hassle for me to have to put things back together that I had spent so much time getting just right in the first place. I hated the goons who turned my place upside down. I was imagining their lives falling apart in mysterious ways because they messed with *The Force of Luke*. Fantasizing my revenge was a more practical approach for now. I needed more practice being a spy before I mixed it up with the pros. I was a smart guy more than a tough guy and did my best to *avoid* fistfights.

Candy and I got me set up to get paid next Friday, which would add some abundance to my new life. It was a blessing to have more money coming in with all that had been destroyed in the past forty-eight hours.

I took a walk on the beach to clear my head. The wind was strong and steady. The surf was big and loud. I never tired of that thunder. There were only a few people at the beach as far as you could see. Every day felt like summer here, but most beach-goers found something else to do after Labor Day. I loved having the beach to myself in the middle of a metropolis. It was an important source of peace and renewal.

The afternoon turned into evening, and it was time to get cleaned up for the Club. It would be packed tonight, with some hot new band playing. I didn't work at the Club as much as I used to but I was a proven asset. Johnnie, the owner, liked to have me around on busy nights to keep an eye on the other bartenders and to put out the inevitable fires. There would be thirty or more working tonight if you included the bartenders, the cocktail waitresses, the dining room waitresses, the busboys, the bouncers, the valets, the kitchen staff and the maintenance crew. Then combine that collection of characters with hundreds of people out to have a good time consuming gallons of alcohol and incredibly loud music. Your judgment and your nerve were often put to the test, but the camaraderie with the staff on a busy night made it memorable.

I spent more time being a pit boss than I did making drinks. You had to make sure the regulars had a good time while keeping yourself ready for the troublemakers. Most of the patrons were easy to manage even if they'd had a few too many. Some were great fun. But on a busy night, there were always drugs being added to the mix along with show-offs who wanted you to see their new Colt Mustang, which weighed less than a pound and was about the size of your wallet.

If the crowd was big enough, there was always some tormented soul looking for a fight. It was like their hobby. They never fought over anything meaningful. Typically, one of these lunatics would pick a fight with one of our regulars. We trained our peacekeepers to give the edge to the regulars and then convincingly encourage the troublemakers to go elsewhere for their fight fix.

In the most challenging confrontations, you had to be calm and hyper-aware at the same time. You had to have a sense about what you could get away with. With some guys, you could take a stand and be gently assertive. The really tough hombres were fearless and were going to do whatever they wanted to do. But, I had witnessed that my most sincere requests had an impact. Even fearless tough guys had a heart in there somewhere.

The hours flew by. The Club was packed, as expected. Everybody and everything were pushed to capacity. I was helping a waitress clean up broken glass after some wasted maniac decided he needed to impress his friends by dancing on his table when another waitress put her hand on my shoulder so she could talk directly into my ear over the noise.

"Luke, they need you in the back of the main bar. Something about a gal with huge naked bouncing breasts decided to take off her sweater to let them breathe? That's what some guy just told me anyway." She said it like she was giving me a present. "Good luck with that." I could hear her laughing as she walked away.

"Thanks, I'll check it out." I headed for the main bar. It took a few minutes to find a path through the mass of humanity. Finally, I got to the back corner, which was standing room only and so packed you couldn't see beyond the person in front of you. Then they appeared, two large exquisite bare breasts with their own vivacious personality attached to a pretty young blonde. She was feeling no pain. My guess was that after a few drinks she noticed the action was a little slow and wanted to get more attention from her admirers. I was told this had been going on for a while. The all-male crowd around her were in no hurry to have this gifted gal cover up such perfection.

As I got closer, I could hear the bloke standing next to her asking her what it was like to have such large breasts. That was the kind of scholarly conversation you often got to hear working in a bar.

I felt like a high school gym teacher telling kids to put their clothes back on, but it had to be done.

"Excuse me, miss, could I ask you to put your top back on?"

"What's the matter, don't you think they're sexy?" She pulled her shoulders and arms back to give me a better look. There was a wanting auditory response from every male in the vicinity. Then one of the guys joined in with, "Hey, we think you're sexy, doll!" Another said, "We're in love with you, angel." That was what she wanted to hear.

I smiled a bigger smile this time, hoping that would help. "Miss, I really need you to put your top back on, or I'm going to get in a lot of trouble."

"Hey, everyone seems to like them. I don't see what the problem is." She was slurring every third word or so.

"What's your name, honey?" I said.

"My friends call me Lulu. What's *your* name, handsome?"

"I'm Luke. I'm the manager." That got moans and groans from the crowd.

"Well, Luke the manager…I seem to have lost my sweater." She giggled.

"Will you guys help Lulu find her sweater?" The fellas standing next to her were happy to help and pretended to look around.

Then I heard Lulu mumble the dreaded words of pending disaster.

"I'm not feeling very good," Lulu said quietly. In the next moment, she projectile-vomited all over the joe in front of her, which got a chorus of shock and awe.

The show was over. I gently grabbed Lulu, who was barely able to stand, and had to hold my breath, the rancid smell was so intense. I took off my blazer and wrapped it around her and headed her toward the side door to get her some fresh air. I flagged down a cocktail waitress to get her cleaned up. My guess was Lulu would not remember much of what had just happened. I would. I have to admit, bearing witness to her ample twins was a pleasant rush. I would do my best to block out the tragic ending.

I was making my rounds taking money out of the cash registers to make a deposit in the back office safe. My phone was vibrating. It was Marci. Oh dear, I had forgotten to call her back. She called yesterday, and I had been so preoccupied with Sophia, I totally spaced calling her back. I let it go to voicemail. She was not going to be happy with me. I decided I had better listen to what she had to say.

Luke darling, I called you yesterday and have not heard from you. I had the best sex of my life with you two nights ago. You said you loved me and wanted to take our relationship to another level. Now I'm starting to think that was just the booze talking. You had a lot to drink and my friend Bonnie told me yesterday that you hit on her by the women's bathroom at the Club. I don't want to believe that, but I don't know what to believe. We need to talk. Please call me.

I needed to figure out what to do with Marci. I liked her. She was really cute and the sex *was* amazing, but she was like most of the women I had dated in recent years. I felt like I was just killing time waiting for my real partner to show up. I would call her now but I had to be available for the next crisis.

"Luke, is that you?"

I turned from the cash register and saw the smiling face of a friend. He was a fifty-something Italian mobster who I had gotten to know at the Club. I had done some small favors for him that seemed harmless. He looked like a million dollars in his black Armani suit and open silk shirt. "Riccardo, how the heck are you? I haven't seen you in a while."

"I'm good. Looks like you're hauling it in tonight."

"Yes, things are jumping. You staying out of trouble?" I said.

"As you know, that's a full-time job for me. Can we talk for a minute?"

"Sure, follow me back to the office."

We walked down a short hall to the kitchen area, which was Grand Central Station. You had to pay attention not to get run over by a waiter or a busboy flying through the double swinging doors. On the opposite side of the kitchen were several small offices. I unlocked the door to the manager's office and motioned Riccardo to follow me.

"Have a seat. I only have a couple of minutes, and we can talk later when things slow down."

"This will just take a minute. I need a small favor. I have a package I need delivered by someone I can count on to *not get caught*. My regular guy got ratted out by an angry ex-girlfriend. There's five grand in it for you. What do you say?"

"Sounds like a generous offer and I could really use the money right now. I need to buy a new car. I don't mind being your alibi on occasion but this is a little different. Do you know what you're delivering?"

"It's better that you don't know. Plausible deniability and all that."

"Those are big words, Riccardo. Where's the drop?"

"It's at a mall close to here. Lots of shoppers. Easy to get lost in the crowd afterwards."

"It sounds easy enough, but not knowing what I'm getting into sounds a bit risky."

"I understand. I'm embarrassed that I even have to ask you for this favor, but I'm in a tough spot. Tell you what, I'll make it ten grand. Does that make it more interesting?"

"That would get me the down on the car I want. It's tempting. All I have to do is drop off a package?"

"You could wear a hoodie or a disguise if you want. You're in, you're out and you get a shiny new black BMW. My favorite color by the way." Riccardo was a salesman.

"Man, it sounds so easy. But that much money means if I get caught I'm into a major legal defense and possible time. Or if someone's watching, which they most likely will be, I'm the next guy they shake down to find out where I got the package. I really hate hospitals. I don't know, Riccardo, I've got some good things happening in my life right now, and I don't want to screw it up. Maybe I should pass. You know what I mean?"

"You in love?" he asked.

"I think I am."

"You *think* you are? You're in love! I can see it in your eyes."

I acknowledged Riccardo's perception with a reserved smile. "Tell you what I *can* do. I know a guy who's good at this sort of thing who might be interested. He's new to town, but I knew him from before. You can trust him."

"I'd rather have *you* do it, but I guess I can check out your guy. With you being in love and all." Riccardo gave me the *I know what it's like* look.

"Here's his name and cell. You can use my name to get in the door but that's it. Keep me out of this. You promise?" I held the piece of paper away from him until I got a promise.

"Okay, my friend. You got it."

I handed Riccardo the name and number. "If my guy works out, I wouldn't mind a little thank-you. The woman I'm in love with likes to spend money."

"Don't they all!" said Riccardo. "Don't worry, I'll take care of you."

"Good luck with your drop. Sounds like a good payday."

"Let's hope so. Later." Riccardo managed to make his way through the double doors and disappeared into the noisy mob.

The crowd had thinned considerably by midnight. Johnnie pulled me aside and said he appreciated me being there for the prime-time avalanche and that he would close if I wanted to take off. That was my signal to check in with Sophia. She was in my thoughts. I could feel a connection with her even if I wasn't consciously thinking about her, and I liked that feeling.

Otherwise, I was glad to be so busy that evening. I needed the distraction from dealing with all the things that were recently broken or destroyed in my world.

I squeezed a lime into an ice-cold Corona and headed for a quiet place in the back of the Club.

"Hey, Luke here, checking in."

"I had a feeling I might hear from you about now," said Sophia. "Can you get away?"

"I'm done. I'm taking my first break of the evening and having a cold one."

"Sounds like it was busy."

"Barely room to move for almost four hours."

"Does that mean you broke up some fights and saved a few damsels in distress?"

"Totally. We had a little bit of everything tonight. But it was fun. No injuries, no arrests, no flashing lights, all in all a good night."

"So are you wired?"

"Mostly I'm excited about seeing you...if you're up for that. I know it's late. How are *you* feeling?"

"I'm good. I'm home, powering down with a glass of wine, answering a few emails. Why don't you just come over here?"

"Where do I go?"

"I live at The Shores in Santa Monica on the beach, 2700 Nielsen Way, number 1502. Just pull in the main entrance and the valet will park your car."

"I know the place. On my way."

Oh, yeah, I needed to call Marci. What to say? I wanted to leave a voicemail rather than get into a conversation. I wanted to get to Sophia's.

It was late, but she knew I worked late and might have her phone on. I called from a number at the Club that I knew said Unknown, hoping she would not pick up. It worked.

Marci, Luke here. I'm really sorry for not getting back to you sooner. I got a job offer that required hours of interviews and then I got the job and they wanted me to start right away. Plus I still have my other two jobs. I've barely been to my apartment other than to change clothes. Give me another day or so and I will tell you all about it. You are in my thoughts. I want to see you as soon as I can. Bye for now.

That would buy me a little time. Sophia, here I come.

I had been to The Shores to play tennis. There were six well-maintained courts on the beach with a teaching pro. This was a pricey high-rise apartment complex right at the center of Santa Monica with spectacular views of the Pacific and the endless city lights at night. There was more than one noteworthy restaurant within walking distance in every direction. Having Sophia live in such a prime location just added to my feeling of excitement. I was even more eager to see her and her place.

I found the elevator and pushed 15, which was the top floor. I had lived in high-rises. Fifteen floors up was an awesome view, especially when there were no other tall buildings nearby.

As I stepped out of the elevator toward 1502, I was headed for the ocean, so I knew she was going to have a view of the water and the city lights toward the South Bay. I had gone without a view of the city lights for years, and I did miss it.

Once at 1502, I quietly knocked. The door opened and my eyes were instantly drawn to the warmth of her eyes and welcoming smile.

"Hey, you found me. Come on in," she said. A dark blue, one-piece workout suit, made of fancy fabric, was a flawless fit. There was a bright orange Pepperdine Waves logo above her left breast, and she was barefoot. Her toenails were a work of art with bright orange polish that matched the Pepperdine logo. Looking at her was always a profound experience for me.

"Thank you." I decided to be on the quiet side and let her lead.

"Make yourself at home. Can I get you something? I've got beer, wine, sparking water, coffee, tea… What sounds good?"

"What are you having?"

"I opened a bottle of Pinot Grigio."

"My favorite." I looked out at the view. "Your place is breathtaking, just like you."

She gave me an enticing smile as she handed me a glass of Pinot. "You seem pretty calm and relaxed after being the host of L.A.'s biggest drunken bash for the past few hours."

"The contrast between there and here is beyond words. But that was then, and this is now. I'm just happy to be here with you at your place. Sometimes when I'm with you, I feel like I'm in a dream. You are definitely real and you are a dream at the same time."

"I like you, too…and I'm glad you're here."

I looked into her eyes, deciding not to say anything and just soak in the joy of the moment.

"When we talked earlier you said you wanted to spend more time getting to know each other and not just talk about work," she said. "The word you used was *hang* if I remember correctly."

"Yes, I want to hang with you."

"Let me tell you what I would like to do, and then we will hear from you. Fair enough?"

"Very democratic," I said.

"I have a huge day tomorrow like I always do. I need to get *some* sleep. I don't think this is our night to drink too much and make love until the sun comes up. How do you feel about that?"

"Well, of course I'm disappointed." I gave her my best disappointed look while trying not to smile.

"I was afraid of that. Have you been imagining what it would be like to make love to me?" She was being artfully clinical.

"Actually, I've had that thought quite often, but I usually have to fight it off and stay focused on whatever we're doing at the time."

"Indeed, one of your many talents and another reason why we can be such an awesome team. Your restraint and ability to focus are greatly appreciated. It is very arousing and sensual to feel how attracted you are to me. But I think you would be surprised at how exciting it is to me that you can focus and skillfully get the job done no matter what we are doing. I love sex, but it isn't more important than being successful.

"We both know that if you act on every impulse, it'll be fun for a while, but eventually it creates more of a mess than a dance. I would rather have us be gifted dancers. What do you think of that idea?"

"Hey, I like to dance. I think I'd do almost anything if it meant being close to you."

"Hmm. Grab your glass and come over here and sit next to me. I want us to feel the energy we get from just touching. You don't have to have sex to feel each other."

I got up from the chair and sat down next to her on the couch. We were then looking out the wide front glass doors together.

"I like sitting next to you," I said. "I like touching you. And I also like to look at you when we talk."

"Good point. Let's face each other and just make sure we are touching somewhere." Our legs were touching and she had gently put her hands on my leg. "You feel that energy?" she said.

"I do. It's astounding. I feel more energy with you than I have ever felt with any woman."

"There's a reason for that which I will tell you about later. It's not important now. Just take it all in."

"Okay." I could barely speak. Usually I found it easy to produce a clever comeback to most anything. I was so mesmerized from just touching this beautiful creature, the thinking part of my brain went to sleep.

"Now I want you to try something else. Are you willing to experiment with me a little?" she said.

"Yes," was all I could say.

"Hold my hands like this. Put your fingers between my fingers. Now relax your hands and your arms and close your eyes. I want you to create a vision with me. I want you to imagine that there is a protective layer over your heart. Just make it up in your mind however you want. Can you see it?"

97

"Got it."

"Now, I want you to pull away the protective layer in front of your heart just for a few minutes. You can put it back anytime. I'm going to do the same thing. Then when it feels right, I want you to beam love from your heart to my heart." She took my hand and put it on her left breast. "Right here. Can you feel that? I mean can you feel my heart?" She was quietly laughing at what she had said.

"Oh yeah," I said.

"Okay, send love from your heart to mine and I'm going to send my love energy back to you."

Everything got quiet. I was visualizing sending love from my heart to her heart. She held my hand to her breast. Then it happened. I felt the most intense rush of warmth and love I had ever felt around my own heart. I was totally still. I didn't want to move for fear the feeling would go away. Then I could feel tears slowly streaming down my cheeks.

I didn't know what else to do so I just kept going. Several times, I consciously focused on sending energy back to her, but then I realized I didn't have to do anything other than to be open to her. The love coming from her was overpowering.

"Okay, you can open your eyes," she said.

My eyes opened and there she was, as radiantly beautiful as ever with tears running down her cheeks.

"Hold me?" she said.

I pulled her toward me and put my arms around her. She put her arms around my neck. We quietly held each other for several minutes. The surge coming from her was like nothing I had ever experienced. I decided to let her make the next move. Finally, I heard her voice. "We have to stop meeting like this."

We both broke out in intense laughter. I hadn't laughed that hard in a long time. All the steam that had been building up inside of us was looking for a release. When we let it go, it was so extreme and so complete.

"You okay?" she said.

"I'm good. I'm more than good. I'm so blown away by you." I could barely talk. I could not stop my tears. Having tears of joy was not something I seemed to have any control over. This was all new to me. "Sorry, I can't seem to talk yet."

"That's okay, honey, take your time."

We sat there on the couch in silence just holding each other. Neither one of us wanted it to end. Finally, I felt like I could speak again. I could tell she was waiting for *me* to take the lead.

"I should probably let you get some sleep," I said.

"I could sleep. In fact, I think I'm going to sleep way better than usual tonight. How about you?"

"Now that you mention it, I'm feeling like I had a big day," I said.

"All right, let's do it." She gently rose from the couch. "Let me walk you to the door, then I need to crash."

She grabbed my hand and helped pull me up. When we got to the door, I put my arms around her again and gave her a long hug. She pulled back slightly and looked into my eyes.

"I want you to kiss me, but I just want a soft kiss. I want a tender 'I care about you' kiss, not a passionate kiss. I need to go to sleep."

"Close your eyes," I said. I gently put my hands on her cheeks and pulled her lips to mine. It was a soft kiss that went longer than I expected. An ideal end to an incredible interlude with my new friend. "See you tomorrow."

"Call me. I don't want to think," she said.

As I closed the door behind me, I could see a big sleepy smile with a hint of "thank you" peeking through. "Thank you" was right. Thank you, God, for Sophia!

10. Jean Claude's Invitation...

Sophia called at 8:05 a.m.

"Do you have plans this evening?" she asked.

"Nothing I can't change with a phone call or two," I said.

"Excellent. We'll be entertaining a special guest this evening. One of my big bosses is here from Paris. I didn't think he was going to be here until tomorrow, but he's here now and wants to have dinner. I thought I would show off my latest secret weapon."

"Okay. You'll have to bring me up to speed."

"It's *you*, silly. You're my secret weapon."

"Of course...I knew that."

"Do you have a tux?" She was in a fanciful mood.

"I do, but it's more of a working tux for being a maître d', and it's at the cleaners."

"How about a dark suit and a dark silk turtleneck?"

"I have both."

"That'll work. Diego will pick you up at your place at seven and then come and get me. We've been invited to dine at the exclusive La Crème Doux at the Hotel Bel-Air." She sounded like she was narrating the old TV show *Lifestyles of the Rich and Famous*.

Oohs and ahs could be heard from the peanut gallery as she described our elegant evening. I was psyched.

"You've got the rest of the day to do whatever you need to do. I know the list is longer than usual with recent disasters. Take some time to be in good spirits for tonight. I need you at your best. You'll be meeting Jean Claude Chartrand, who is a force of nature. I will tell you more about him when you pick me up."

I got the impression tonight was a big deal and she was taking a bit of a risk bringing me along. But I knew it must feel right to her or she wouldn't have asked me.

"I'll be ready." I was more serious than usual.

"I know you will." When she spoke to you, you felt like you were the most important person in the world to her.

"The line of people who need to see me is getting longer by the minute, so let's save our time together for tonight," she said.

"I'm all for that!"

Most of the day was spent online buying items for the apartment. I took a break and went to the BMW dealership and drove a couple of cars. I wasn't ready to buy. Then I got really inspired on the way home and met Marci for coffee and had a heart-to-heart.

I really did care about Marci. She was a sweetheart and an ideal companion for the old me. I couldn't tell her much about my new life but I did my best to break the news gently. I told her I had an unusual opportunity that was going to take all my free time for the indefinite future, and that wouldn't be fair to her. I said I would be in training for six months and if they did take me, I wasn't even sure where I would live. She was disappointed, but happy for me, which I knew she would be. She was a giver. We hugged and kissed and said our tearful goodbyes, which was harder for me than I had anticipated. There was a part of me that did not want to say goodbye to Marci, but I knew it was the right thing to do.

I worked out at the gym and did a few laps at the pool to clear the cobwebs. With my tailored black suit and dark burgundy silk turtleneck, I was ready for anything. A fancy night out with my new friend and her big boss was next. I would be escorting a gorgeous, important woman, who liked having me around, to dinner at one of the most exclusive restaurants in Los Angeles. I couldn't have dreamed it any better.

Diego texted that he was waiting out front. I had learned from a previous ride with Diego that he was a man of few words and as strong as an ox. The iron grip of his handshake was a clue in addition to his linebacker shoulders and wide neck. It wouldn't surprise me if he was trained to protect Sophia. He was confident about his job in an unimposing way. Eager to serve with a great smile. I could see why Sophia liked him.

We pulled up to The Shores. Time to pick up Cinderella— or maybe I was the one who turned into a pumpkin at midnight. Oops, I needed to maintain a positive vision and make the best of this fairy tale.

"Knock, knock. Are you decent?" I slowly opened the door and heard her distant voice say to come in and help myself to anything I wanted. I wasn't ready for a drink, so I headed toward the balcony door, which was open. There wasn't a breath of wind and the surf had been big again today. The sun was thinking about calling it a day as it watched over the smooth silver-blue expanse of the Pacific. There was something primal about watching a massive wave slowly swell to its biggest potential and then crash with all its power.

"Hey, you." Sophia walked out onto the balcony. "Enjoying the view?"

"Immensely. You look stunning."

"Thank you. So do you. Will you hook me?"

She turned her back to me. Her hair was fancier than usual, which meant really fancy. It was pulled back in the front with long flowing curls in the back down to her shoulders. She was wearing an elegant long taupe dress that shimmered as she moved. There was a slit in the front that was well above her knees. One bare shoulder, one covered, long sleeves and I couldn't help notice her legs and her shoes. I usually didn't pay much attention to women's shoes, but these were black open-toed high heels with delicate leather crisscrossing straps. She was ready for the red carpet at the Oscars. And she smelled great. Perfume was usually a deal breaker for me. Whatever she was wearing in that department was subtle and seductively pleasant.

"Let me get my shawl and purse and I'm ready."

"After you..."

She pulled the apartment door closed. I extended my arm, which she willingly accepted with a beaming smile.

As we got to the elevator she said, "Don't push the button yet. I need to tell you a couple things about Jean Claude before we get downstairs."

I gently let go of her arm and faced her so we could talk.

"He is charming and charismatic. You will like him. He is diabolically smart, as intuitive as anyone I have ever met and he has a profound spiritual connection. One more thing, he's a billionaire with a *B*."

"Oh, is that all?"

She put her hand on my arm and gave me the *stay with me* look.

"I usually meet with the board as a group, occasionally in person, but usually on a conference call. In the past, when Jean Claude has asked to see me alone, he's had big news of some kind. My feeling is that something important is happening and it looks like he's willing to include you in whatever the news is. So I need to ask you to do something for me."

"Of course. Name it."

"I need you to see yourself as a much bigger player in this game than you have so far. You are doing exceedingly well with your orientation and I know this program is a lot to take in, but Jean Claude doesn't do anything in a small way. He likes to throw people into jobs way over their head and see how they do. He has already done that to me more than once and I have managed to make it work. That's how I got the job I have.

"He knows you have passed my test and that I want you around. I'm sure that's why you were invited to dinner tonight. But it also means that you could be offered more responsibility than you could ever imagine. I need you to be ready for that possibility and to respond appropriately."

"That is fascinating and a little scary. I guess I'm not sure what *respond appropriately* means."

"It means to not be intimidated by the magnitude of what he's up to, or what he's in charge of or the resources he has. Jean Claude represents the biggest players in the game on a worldwide scale, and you may be invited to sit at the table. That could feel like a big jump from nightclub manager by night, financial advisor by day. I see you as much more capable than you do because I see who you really are. I need you to trust my perception until we've had more time to give you more proof that you can do it."

"What an outrageous and wonderful request. I think I'm in love."

That got a tender smile, but she wasn't deterred.

"So can you do that for me? Can you act as if you're a bigger player? Imagine yourself as that person. Be that person right now and you *are* that person. Actually, we are making up who we think we are right now anyway. It's all in our heads to a great degree. I'm just asking you to make up who you think you are a little differently."

"When you say it that way it sounds easy."

"It *is* easy. I've seen you do it."

"If I do this, do I get to ask for something?"

"Ah, Negotiator Guy has joined us."

"You know what I want," I said.

"I have some ideas about that, but I better let you tell me so I don't make the wrong assumptions."

"I want time alone with you to hang out and be together without the job description."

"Okay, but you know the drill. It has to be spontaneous, in the flow of everything else. I can't schedule it."

"I can work with that. I trust that if it's on your radar, you'll make it happen."

"Come on, honey." She pulled me toward the elevator and pushed the Down button. "It's time to take a ride on the biggest, scariest roller coaster you've ever been on."

I didn't know what to say. And then it occurred to me that I needed to trust my intuitive instincts like never before. Tonight was the night to take it up a notch. Let the games begin. I was feeling bigger already.

After twenty minutes of slow city driving, we were in the Hollywood Hills. The trees were old and majestic. The lawns rolled on forever in all directions. An occasional stone fence or the white picket type you see around horse ranches in Kentucky. Paved driveways taking off from the main road with no house in sight. The houses were there, you just couldn't see them. If you owned a home in this neighborhood, you owned enough land or forest that it was difficult to see your house from the main road.

The sun had set shortly after we left Sophia's apartment. All the roads and driveways looked the same, with very few signs and no streetlights. Eventually we came upon an unpretentious sign that said *Hotel Bel-Air* with an arrow pointing northeast. If you didn't have a GPS, it would be easy to get lost out here. Of course, we had Diego, who was peacefully driving along like he had made the trip many times before.

We reached the entrance to the hotel. A modest old stucco mountain lodge with a red tile roof stood before us, much of which was hidden by big trees and lush foliage. A few lights here and there but much darker than I had expected. Exclusive in this case meant in the middle of the woods on the side of a mountain.

Diego drove up to the main door. We were greeted by a doorman who pointed us down a long covered walkway to the main restaurant. As we walked, we saw gardens and patios backing up to meeting rooms and places for private parties. I had heard this was a popular place for weddings.

Our walk took us to a bridge over a large koi pond with about thirty well-fed colorful fish frolicking in the moonlight. This place was an interesting blend of relaxed luxury and mountain trail—quiet, peaceful and invigorating.

When we arrived at La Crème Doux, there was a rustic lighted wooden case with the menu for the evening just outside the entrance. On the menu was a six-course meal with options for each course. Every item had a gourmet description of how each delicacy was prepared. No prices. I was glad I had been invited to dinner.

As we made our grand entrance, we were welcomed by a maître d'.

"Will you be dining with us this evening?"

"Yes, reservation for Chartrand." Sophia pronounced his name as they would say it in France.

"Monsieur Chartrand is waiting for you at his private table on the Terrace Alcove. Please follow me."

The mood and decor of the restaurant were elegant yet understated. As we approached our table, there was a wall on each side with antique lanterns for light. The back wall had been taken out, opening onto a lush garden with spotlights strategically placed to make you feel like you were eating outside under the stars. It was spectacular.

"*Bonjour, mes amis.*" Jean Claude's voice and demeanor were warm and friendly as he hugged Sophia. He was in his fifties, tall and fit-looking, with sandy brown hair, lots of freckles and impeccably dressed in a dark brown pinstripe suit with a beige shirt and matching tie. "You look particularly sensational tonight, *mademoiselle*. My guess is that it may have something to do with your handsome beau." He extended his hand.

"I'm Luke Lamaire. It's my pleasure."

"Jean Claude Chartrand. And you are of French heritage. I knew you must be special to win the attention of the accomplished Sophia."

"That's very kind of you, *merci*."

"Sophia tells me you are her *arme secrète*."

"Secret weapon, *oui*, that is what she calls me."

Jean Claude looked at Sophia. "I like this one already. Please...sit. Chef Vincens claims he has been cooking all afternoon for us. He assures me this will be his *pièce de résistance*."

"I can hardly wait to see what he has prepared," said Sophia.

The waiter uncorked a bottle of red wine with a fancy French label. He poured a small amount in a wineglass for Jean Claude to taste and approve. He nodded to the waiter and said, "*Trés bien*."

"Luke, I hope you don't mind that this is a working dinner. My schedule is full and I want to make the most of our time together," he said.

"You're in charge," I said.

"Wonderful," he said. "So Sophia... Am I to assume that you have made your choice and Luke here is our man?"

"Yes."

"And you trust him with your life?"

"Yes."

"Does he have a clearance?"

"Not officially—that is forthcoming. He has been briefed on the basics of the LightSpace Project but not in great detail."

"I will proceed as if he has the highest clearance. That's the only way to do this. We have no time to waste. I trust your judgment."

"I agree," said Sophia.

"Luke, I would like to tell you a story that only a handful of people know. As Sophia has told you, we are not alone in the Universe. There are many other forms of intelligent life much closer to us than you might expect. We have advanced much faster with our technology than with our enlightenment. Soon we will have the ability to travel at warp speed, which will allow us to travel anywhere in the galaxy and beyond.

"There is a group of intelligent beings—let's call them ETs—who are in charge of regulating the planets that achieve warp speed or anything similar that would allow space travel. Their mission is to keep any war-prone species from achieving space travel. In other words, in our galaxy, there are no star wars. The more advanced species won't allow it, and they have formidable power. Their technology is beyond our comprehension. Are you with me so far?"

"Yes. Sophia has told me much of what you've said."

"Good. So here is where it gets interesting. We are being given a chance to evolve to a level where we will be allowed to have space travel. First, we must prove that we can become peace-loving spirits rather than war-prone egos. If we prove that we can be a safe addition to the Universal community, we get our wings. If we fail to evolve to their satisfaction, humans will be erased as a failed experiment.

"We are considered too dangerous and too far along with our technology to be allowed to propagate our species *and* have space travel. Since we have polluted and destroyed a good part of our home planet, the assumption is that we will do the same wherever we go. It also doesn't help that our primary solution to international disputes is war or the threat of war. The Galactic Confederation of Planets has a *no-tolerance* policy toward war or any kind of violence. What do you think of that?"

"Sounds like a plot for a sci-fi movie to me." I wanted to lighten things up a little.

"Yes, it does sound like science fiction, but it's all quite real."

108

"So what happens next?" I asked.

"We have to get a critical mass of our Planetary Leaders to reach lightspace."

"What are Planetary Leaders?"

"Sophia will bring you up to speed on those details. For the sake of this conversation, let's just say they are the candidates most likely to want to achieve lightspace. The good news is that we don't need everyone to reach lightspace. If we get enough—or a critical mass, which is the scientific term—the rest of the population will automatically shift to the higher state of being."

"Like the monkeys that learned to peel bananas," I said.

"Exactly like that," said Jean Claude. "Sophia, do you know the story about how monkeys learned to peel bananas?"

"No, I must have skipped class that day and gone to the beach."

Jean Claude smiled at Sophia before he continued. "As the story goes, there were research scientists studying monkeys in a variety of locations around the world. Apparently, monkeys didn't always eat bananas—at least they didn't peel them. But somehow a group of smart monkeys on an island somewhere figured out how to peel bananas so they could eat the good part and not the skin. Then an amazing thing happened. All at once, monkeys all over the world started to peel their bananas and only eat the fruit and not the peel."

"I wish it were that easy. And speaking of eating," said Sophia, "I think they want to know if we are ready to start with dinner."

"Ah, *mais oui*, let's have some of the exquisite food we've been promised," said Jean Claude. "We can continue our conversation. Just be aware of the wait staff. They have been instructed to minimize the interruptions and not to linger."

For the first time, I realized there were two conservatively dressed men in dark suits keeping an eye on things from a distance who were not part of the wait staff. Bodyguards were becoming a regular part of my life.

The conversation shifted to lighter fare while we were served several courses of our six-course meal. The food was beautifully prepared and presented. Small servings of one delicacy after another with many new tastes and seasonings. It was great fun. Sophia and Jean Claude were comfortable enough to tease each other in a playful way, but they both had an intensity underneath the surface that driven people have. Now that we had food to eat for a while, I expected Jean Claude to get back to business.

"So Luke, what do you think about lightspace?"

"It sounds like a Utopia."

"It *is* a Utopia for the individual and a community of any size. Let me tell you a little more about our project and where you fit in.

"There is a core group who have achieved lightspace. The training was actually done by the ETs with their advanced technology. We can't tell you any more than that for now. We know you'll have lots of questions. The training experience was quite incredible, to say the least. There are several small groups around the world who have been helped to achieve lightspace and have been assigned the job of finding Planetary Leaders and then helping them reach lightspace. You will learn more about the groups, but for now all you need to know is that Sophia and I are part of one group and Sophia has a counterpart in London and New York. Everyone is working together to develop a program to reach lightspace as quickly as possible so we can evolve as a species.

"You, my friend, are the first candidate to be selected for the LightSpace Training on the West Coast."

"Me! I'm the first candidate!? You mean you don't have any other graduates?" I had to remind myself to close my mouth a couple of times, I was so stunned.

"Not yet," said Jean Claude. "Right now the only graduates are those of us who have been trained by the ETs. Now it is our job to continue that training and develop our own approach. We have been given a boost by helpful outsiders.

Now we have to figure out how to make it work on our own. We have to take off the training wheels and learn to ride the bike without any outside assistance."

I looked at Sophia. "What about all those people at ASC that I met the other night?"

"They are all part of a movement for better communication," she said. "Which is a perfect cover for us and a perfect platform to recruit from. But they don't know all the things we are telling you. You are part of an elite group at the very beginning stages. We are a brand-new baby."

"How did you two get selected out of all the people in the world to do this? That is amazing all by itself. And how did *I* get on the short list!?"

"Imagine how we must feel to be given this opportunity and to have seen what we have seen," said Jean Claude. "This is the biggest challenge ever given to human beings. We have to make this work or we all get the *guillotine*. The answer to your question is that you will know everything in time. Be patient. We had to go through the same process that you are going through."

"Unbelievable," I said.

"Sophia, my dear, how is your entrée?" asked Jean Claude.

"It is delectable. Thank you for asking." She looked at me and smiled like she was proud of me.

"So you guys are Columbus, and I'm the first-mate-in-training?"

"Something like that," said Jean Claude. "Are you ready to learn how to reach your greatest possible human potential and then help us teach others how to do it and save the world and the human race in the process?"

"Well sure, I already signed up but I didn't realize I was going to be the tip of the spear. I'm the new Marines. I lead the attack. What if I fail? I would have the *dis-honor* of being the biggest and final failure in the history of humans!"

"You can do it," said Jean Claude. "Sophia and I both did it. We will help you. As long as you don't give up, we have a good chance to make it."

"A good chance to make it!? How do you handle the pressure? It must be overwhelming."

"You will have lots of questions—that's normal. The good news is that when you reach lightspace, you have exponentially more power to create whatever you want in your life. To us, this is just what there is to do. We have been chosen to do this work. We are honored to be chosen, we will give it our best effort, and we expect to succeed even if we don't know exactly how yet. What we *do* know is that you are part of the solution if you want to be."

"How do you know that? And how can you be so calm about all this!?" My analytical mind was horrified.

Sophia put her hand on my arm to calm me. It worked instantly. That was amazing. That wasn't normal. When she touched me, I became more peaceful and more intelligent all at once.

"Let's have some dessert and coffee," said Sophia.

As I let it all sink in, I felt embarrassed. I was sitting with two of the most gifted leaders on planet Earth, who wanted my help, and I was obsessed that I might screw up my part and be the cause of the end of the human race. I *was* being the weak link that Sophia had asked me not to be. Had I considered that those who had been chosen to save the species would not just pick anyone to help them? Would I be willing to see myself as a person of importance in this staggering challenge?

"I think I need an *Irish* coffee." I got a knowing smile from both of my new comrades.

11. Tennis Anyone?

The evening with Jean Claude was a success. The new world order just got its first candidate for lightspace school on the West Coast, Luke "Not So Fast" Lamaire. We said our goodbyes until the next time. Jean Claude had to get to another meeting in downtown L.A. Then he mentioned he had a somewhat unusual request. He asked me if I would mind if Sophia went with him. He said that having her at his meeting would make it much more difficult for the other guys to play hardball, which he was expecting. He said, "Let her be *my* secret weapon and I will owe you one." I said, "Of course."

Giving up my prom date for the evening was disappointing but it felt like the right thing to do. Although I suspected that Sophia and Jean Claude had been more than just business partners, I didn't really have much of a choice. It then occurred to me that my competition for Sophia included billionaires, celebrities, heads of state and probably leaders of other planets—and that was just the super-powerful contenders.

As we did our casual hugs to say goodnight, she whispered in my ear that I got major points for this gesture. I reminded her that the way she looked, there would be jaws dropping wherever she went. She acknowledged my compliment with a kiss on my cheek. That further confirmed I had made the right choice. And I was right, the two large gentlemen in dark suits at the restaurant left with Jean Claude and Sophia in *his* stretch limo.

When I woke up the next morning I had the feeling that the day was right for a new car, and sure enough within a few hours I found myself riding along the coast with my sunroof open listening to iTunes Radio. I went back to the local BMW dealership and made a deal on a two-year-old 328i. It had very low miles and was owned by a little old lady who had barely used it, according to the salesman. The car was actually in such mint condition that the story might have actually been true. Whatever the story, it was a beauty.

Incoming. It was Sophia. "Hey there."

"Luke, what are you up to?"

"I'm driving around in my new car."

"Wonderful news. I can't wait to see it. What did you get?"

"Oh, I like BMWs. I got another 328i."

"What color is it?"

"Black metallic."

"That's a great car for you. Are you happy?"

"Yes. It's the end of the month and they made me a decent offer."

"I have good news as well. How would you like to play tennis with me?"

"Tennis is one of my favorite things. Is this work or play?"

"It's mostly play but there's a work element. Tennis is an excellent way to teach you about lightspace, and since you play, we should use it as part of your training."

"I like that idea. How good are you?" I asked.

"You're gonna find out soon enough."

"That's a lot of confidence for a *girl* with *orange* toenails."

"Trash talking already. I'm afraid you won't be able to see my toenails today, baby doll, only the blur of my fancy footwork!"

"I can't think of anything I'd rather watch."

"Oh, that's right. You're a lover not a fighter. We'll see how that works for you out on the court."

"Man, you're a tough cookie. So when does this grudge match begin?"

"How soon can you be here?" she asked.

"I'm close."

"Hurry on over. I've got balls."

"You certainly do!"

She waited for me to stop chuckling. "It's a good thing you're cute. Bye-ee."

What a neat development that was. There was nothing I would rather do for exercise than play tennis. If I could learn how to do lightspace by playing tennis, that would be ideal for me. I was going to have to really focus on my game. She was distracting to me when she was fully clothed and stationary, let alone running around all sweaty in a tiny tennis outfit. To me, there was nothing sexier than an attractive woman who could unload on a tennis ball. I learned a lot the other day when Sophia helped me with my telephone approach. She had said that lightspace is about how you live life and the best way to learn it is to do challenging things. This was a challenge I was looking forward to!

I pulled into the main entrance of The Shores and reluctantly gave my car keys to the valet. I felt lucky to have scored this car and didn't want anything to happen to my new baby. The dealership had given me a valet key but I'd left it at the apartment. I was being overly protective but was still emotionally unsettled from the recent calamities in my life. Let a few weeks pass without any new catastrophes and I would feel better.

The courts were often windy in the afternoon. Today was no exception. The dark green windscreens on all the fences helped. There was a little office and pro shop at the other end, which was Court One. That is usually where the resident pro teaches and there are often a few bleachers for observers. I could see a woman with a long dark ponytail talking to someone behind the counter. I suspected that was my competition for the afternoon, so I headed in that direction.

"There you are," said Sophia. "Don, this is my friend Luke. Don is the pro here. He was telling me that they just replaced all of the nets so they're back to regulation height."

"I hope that doesn't hurt your game," said Don as he looked at me with an impish grin.

"So you're on her side already. I see how this works."

"Well, she's the prettiest and the most talented female player we have around here, so I try to take care of her. There are a lot of young girls who want to play tennis as well as she does, which keeps me busy giving lessons."

"She is an inspiration to us all," I said.

"I don't have a lesson until four," said Don. "You can have the court for two hours. I'll be here if you need anything."

"Thanks, Don," said Sophia. We headed out onto the court.

"You look ready for action," I said. As I had suspected, Sophia was a sight to behold. She had on a tiny black tennis skirt with a bright orange sleeveless half-top that exposed her curvy sculpted abs which would definitely challenge my concentration. Maybe that was part of her strategy. Her orange visor matched her top. I was going to comment that her top matched her toenails but I decided to save that for later. I needed to find out how good she was.

"Let's do this," she said. "I'm ready for a workout."

"And I see you have orange balls. I don't think I have ever played with orange balls."

"You're going to do a lot of things with me that you've never done before."

"Touché."

We started to hit. She had a smooth stroke and knew how to get in position to hit a high-percentage shot. She had a big follow-through that gave her power. Women usually needed to use their body more because they don't have the upper arm strength that men have. She was more graceful than I had anticipated. This was really fun already.

"So how does this work?" I asked.

"Let's hit for a while to get warmed up and then we can experiment a little."

"Sounds good."

We hit for about fifteen minutes. She was a ball machine. She wasn't going for winners but she was making me move around the court. She was a pleasure to hit with. I was getting a great workout.

"Let's try a couple of little things you can focus on to increase your concentration and skill level." She walked toward the net. I followed suit.

"I want you to concentrate on not looking to see where you hit the ball until after you finish your follow-through. It's harder than it sounds. You have good coordination and you don't have to watch the racquet hit the ball most of the time."

"So you want me to watch the racquet hit the ball and not look to see where the ball is going until after I finish my follow-through."

"Exactly. Try that and see what happens."

She hit an easy volley to my forehand. I hit it back but I didn't see the ball hit the racquet.

"Try again," she said.

She hit another easy volley to my forehand. I turned and took my racquet back to get ready, then watched the racquet hit the ball and followed through without looking up. "That felt a little weird."

"Yes, and you hit a shot that was hard for me to get. Did you think about where you were hitting the ball?"

"Kind of. I was just trying to hit it over and not out."

"Okay. So this time, let's do the same shot and imagine the court in your mind. Pretend you can see exactly where the court is in your mind's eye and that you don't have to look to know where to aim the shot."

She hit me the same easy shot. I got ready and hit the ball and didn't look, except this time I imagined hitting into the corner to my left, her right.

"Nice shot! How'd that feel?"

"It still feels weird because I am so used to looking to see how I did rather than trusting my mind to know where the court is," I said.

"That's right. I can't speak for the pros but for solid recreational tennis players, if you watch the racquet hit the ball and see in your mind where you want the ball to go, you will hit a good shot the majority of the time."

"And why is that?" I asked.

"As soon as you hit the shot, your analytical mind is obsessed with judging and evaluating how you did. The problem is, that's the wrong focus for playing your best tennis. Your analytical mind is stealing your attention away from your ability to hit the ideal shot.

"Your right brain knows exactly where the court is and where the lines are without looking. You have hit tens of thousands of tennis balls. Your analytical mind has no idea where the court is unless it looks. That's why you want to look to see how you did as soon as you hit the shot.

"If I see someone looking to see how they did on each shot as soon as they hit the ball, I know I can most likely beat them. Sure, they can be lucky for a while, but the longer we play, the more shots they are going to miss and the more shots I am going to make because I have a better chance of hitting the optimal shot each time."

"How do you define the optimal shot?" I asked.

"It's a shot away from your opponent so you make them work but not so close to the line that you risk hitting it out or hitting the net."

"So that's the way you play all the time?"

"Yep, and I'm hard to beat. Even big guys with lots of muscle will hit enough unforced errors that I can beat them. Although sometimes I let them win. It depends on how much I like them." She tilted her head forward so she could look at me above her sunglasses and awaited my response.

"I can see you've given this game a lot of thought."

"Now if a powerful guy is using his intuition to hit the ball like I'm describing, he's going to be a lot more competition for me," she said.

"You're right. You hit the ball back with a higher percentage than I do. I miss slightly more shots than you do. I think I can hit more winners than you, but what you're saying is you *want* me to go for winners because I'm going to miss half of those shots if I'm hitting with my analytical mind."

"If you watch a professional tennis match and study the shots they miss, they are looking at *where* they want to hit the ball and not *at the ball* while visualizing where the court is in their mind."

"Fascinating. Let's hit some more."

"Actually, let's play. What I'm describing is much more obvious when you play for points. You serve."

I took some practice serves. I hit a few in and hit the net half the time like I always did. I liked to hit the ball hard when I served. It just felt good.

"Now do the same thing with your serve. Don't look to see if the serve is good or not until after you have completed your follow-through. Also, don't hit so hard. Back off 10-15 percent. Not a lot, just some."

I hit a serve and it hit the tape right at the very top of the net.

"What is the last thing you saw after you hit the ball?"

"The net. How did you know that?"

"That's your analytical mind," she said. "It's obsessed with knowing how you did. And if you let it watch, you're going to miss half of your first serves."

I served again, except this time I kept my eyes focused on watching the racquet hit the ball and following through without looking to see if the serve was good. I was actually trying to stay focused on the spot in the air where I hit the ball until I finished my follow-through.

"Ace! That was as good as you can hit a serve right in the corner of the box with decent speed. If you can hit a serve like that and alternate back and forth from one corner to the other, you can give anybody major problems with your serve."

"Let me take a few more. I want to make sure this isn't dumb luck."

"Remember, the hardest thing to do is to not look to see if the serve is good. You will hit a perfect serve by not looking, and then on the next serve you will totally forget that's what you did and go back to the old way."

I hit the next serve and it hit the tape.

"What was the last thing you saw?" she said.

"The net, and it was only a flash. I barely saw it."

"Your analytical mind is sneaky. It will make you look and then try to convince you that it didn't look. But if you remember the last thing you saw when you hit a good serve, it won't be the net. If you do it right, your analytical mind won't have any idea if the serve was in or not, but your intuition knows."

"How does your intuition know if it was a good serve?"

"You can feel it. You actually know what it feels like to hit a serve in, but we ignore that feeling in favor of looking to see how we did each time. When you don't look, you are like a blind person that starts to depend on other senses. When you don't look to see how you did, you automatically use a part of the brain that knows exactly how to hit the serve in, your intuition."

"That is so different than the way we naturally do things," I said.

"And that's the problem. We need to change the way we do things. It is actually more natural to be intuitive but we've been programmed to be more analytical by our academic school system. Let's play a few more points. I want you to really get this," she said.

I served and didn't look. Great serve, and she returned it to my backhand. I looked at where I wanted to hit the ball instead of watching the ball and hit it into the net.

"What happened?" she asked.

"I didn't watch the ball or visualize the court in my mind."

"Good. Really focus this time. See how many times in a row you can see where you want to hit the ball in your mind, watch the racquet hit the ball, and then get ready for the next shot without looking to see if the shot was good or not."

"Got it. 15 love."

I hit another good serve and waited to look. She returned it to my forehand. I turned to the side and took my racquet back and pointed at the ball with my left hand as I hit it. I visualized in my mind where I wanted to hit the ball and then I unloaded on that sucker and didn't look to see where it went.

"Nice shot. Total winner. No way I can get that," she said.

"Amazing. What I just learned is that if you want to play really good tennis you don't get to watch your shots, you focus on hitting the ball and then getting ready for the next shot. It seemed so obvious but hard to remember at the same time."

"You got it. It's just developing new habits." She was pleased.

We played hard for another hour. She was a tough competitor and such a treat to watch. Our games went long, but I was winning 5 to 4 when she looked at her watch.

"This has been fun but I have to get ready to go out," she said. "Let's talk for a few minutes and then I have to go."

We sat on the bench facing the court.

"You played well today," she said.

"Thanks to you. I've never had more fun playing tennis."

"So what did you learn?"

"First I want to know if you let me win."

121

"You already know how much I like you, so what do you think?"

"I'm not sure."

"The match wasn't over. There was no winner today," she said.

"You're very smooth for a girl whose toenails match her outfit."

"How do you know? You can't see my toenails."

"The image is burned into my memory from our last midnight rendezvous."

"So tell me what you learned today," she said.

"I learned that I play better tennis if I trust my intuition to hit the ball rather than using my analytical mind. If I envision the court in my mind as I watch the racquet hit the ball, I hit a much better shot. If I look too soon to see if my shot was good rather than watching the racquet hit the ball, I have let my analytical mind take over and things go downhill from there. And, it takes a lot of concentration to do it consistently. I feel like a beginner in that department. I feel like I have ADD or something."

"You're on the right track. You can't do lightspace until you learn to stop looking to see how you're doing with your analytical mind. Until we learn in our experience that the analytical mind doesn't know what it's doing most of the time, we will continue to use it improperly and suffer the consequences. There's more to it but you're getting the basics."

"When do I see you again?"

"Let's talk late morning tomorrow. Things are crazy busy when Jean Claude is here." She stood, so I did as well.

"How did you two do last night?" I said.

"It was interesting. I was definitely able to help him get a better deal. I actually did some of the negotiating, so it was fun. I'd rather hang out, but I need to run. We will definitely do this again."

"Can I get a hug?"

"I'm all sweaty."

"I know." I gently pulled her toward me and surrounded her heart with love like she had taught me. Then I softly kissed her glistening neck.

"Oh my," she sighed. "We'd better not do any more of that right now or I'll never make it to dinner."

I whispered in her ear, "Thanks for today, coach."

12. The Formula...

"I have several meetings today on the bay patio at the Ritz,"
said Sophia. "I just walked into the hotel. Can you be here in
fifteen minutes?"

"I guess I can force myself to do lunch at the Ritz," I said.
"How will I recognize you?"

"I'll be the one emanating the most love and peace for all
mankind. Close your eyes when you get to the hostess stand
and see if you can feel where I'm sitting."

"Ah, a game of intuitive sensitivity, my favorite."

"Mine too. Get your cute butt over here."

"On my way."

After an expected slow-moving but pleasant drive with sun
on my face and good music, I pulled into the main entrance of
the Ritz to see where I should park. An attendant opened my
car door and asked me how long I was going to be. I was
startled for a second thinking I was going to park the car
myself and then I remembered where I was. I quickly shifted
to a ritzier state of mind and managed to say, "An hour or so."
He said, "*No problema,*" and that he would keep my car
toward the front. I asked if he'd be working all afternoon. He

said, "*Sí*." I introduced myself. His name was Agustin and I especially liked him after he said, "See you after lunch, boss."

As I walked into the massive lobby, I was already warming up my radar for psychically locating my lunch date. I headed for the water, which was straight ahead. When I got close to the hostess stand I closed my eyes to see if I could feel where she was sitting. I got a hit that she was to the left. I couldn't get any more information than that, even with my eyes open. The patio was huge and packed with the lunch crowd. And the umbrellas didn't help.

A middle-aged Asian man meticulously dressed in all black walked up to the hostess stand, checked his reservations, grabbed a couple of menus, and said, "Are you having lunch, sir?"

"Yes, I'm meeting Sophia Forlani."

"Of course, this way, please." He turned and took off, so I decided I had better keep up. We walked briskly across the large patio to the water's edge and then took a left, all the way down to the end. Sophia was good at getting quiet tables in crowded places. I was right. I would be able to report to my intuitive mentor that I could sense where she was as I approached the restaurant. I can't think of anything more fun than this. Well maybe…but I'd better not think about that right now!

There she was in a bright yellow sundress with her hair up and held together with matching yellow chopsticks. She was a picture of perfection. Then it occurred to me that with her radar she knew when I was parking my car so there was no point in acting surprised to see her. Being really happy to see her felt like a better tack.

"What took you so long?" She was obviously teasing.

"Hey, I got here as soon as I could. You look amazing."

"Thank you. I did all this for you. I know how much you like yellow."

"When it comes to your attire I haven't seen a color I didn't like. What a great place to have meetings."

"Yeah, this is as good as it gets around here. This is one of my favorite places to meet people. The office is nice, but it's good to have a change of scenery and I love being outdoors. I have lots to talk about so get yourself settled. Figure out what you want for lunch and then let's get into it."

"Okay. What's good here?" I said.

"It's all good. It really depends on how hungry you are and what you feel like eating. I've never had anything here that wasn't exceptional."

"So many choices."

"So could you sense where I was when you got close to the hostess stand?"

"You will be pleased to know that I had a clear hit of *left* and that's where you turned out to be."

"Good for you. I'm excited to hear that. Not that I doubted you for a second. Do you know what you want for lunch? Tell you what, play along with me. If you could have anything you wanted for lunch, what would it be? This menu is big enough that they probably have it."

"Okay, I'd like a seafood combo of shrimp, crab and lobster with some pasta and a spicy tomato sauce to put on it."

"That's it? That's what you really, really want?"

"Well, I'd rather have an ice-cold Corona with a lime and a shot of Herradura and nothing on my mind but making you giggle. But that probably isn't going to fly for a working lunch."

"Yeah, I know what you mean. That does sound good, though. Rain check?" She was good at saying no in a pleasant way. I needed to improve my skills in that area. "So find something close to what you want on the menu. We can ask them to add the rest. They like me here."

"I'll bet they do... Okay, I see what I want. So what's our goal for this gathering?"

"First, any burning questions? Are we good there for the moment?"

"Yes, the list is long, but it can wait."

"Good. Then let's talk about the formula."

"The formula. I assume this isn't the recipe for Kentucky Fried Chicken or the secret sauce they put on Big Macs."

She laughed. "You're such a guy—or should I say animal? Everything is going through two basic filters—food, and I hate to mention the other one. I want to keep you focused on our work."

"Hey, I'm not like most guys. I do everything for love."

"That's actually quite romantic, but I'm afraid that also leads us away from our current topic," she said. "So let's just say that you can't eat the formula but you will love the formula. It's one of the most effective tools for achieving lightspace."

"Tell me about this formula I'm going to love."

"This is the ideal formula for creating anything you want in this reality. The formula is simple. Stay big picture with me and you'll get it. It's so amazing!"

I sang the first three words of the McCartney song. "Baby, I'm amazed..."

I was going for a smile but she was focused on the formula. This seemed like a big deal to her. I hoped I would be as excited about it as she was.

"The three parts of the formula are *Vision, Action* and *Attitude*. Vision is about imagining what you want to create. A vision can be something you want to happen in the next five minutes or the next five years. It could be for something big like a complex project or something small like what you want for lunch.

"Sometimes visions are complete in every detail and sometimes they can be sketchy. Usually a vision is something you can see. For those who are less visual and more feeling-oriented, the vision can be a sense or a feeling, but since I know you're super visual, let's say our vision is something we can see. You with me so far?"

"I can see it all now," I said.

"Let me keep going." She flashed an effortless smile. "I know you have a vivid imagination but I don't want to hear from that part of you just yet.

"The second part is Action. Once you have a vision, you need to take action in order to bring the vision into reality. How we decide on what action to take is a combination of strategy and tactics based on our experience and the resources available.

"Since the intuitive part of the brain is big picture, you ideally want your intuitive instincts to be your guide in terms of direction and timing. Then you use your analytical mind with its narrow focus to help with the details.

"The masses in our society have been trained to do everything with their analytical mind and ignore the intuition, which makes us very slow, cautious and clumsy. We are trained by our school system to use the slowest part of the brain for everything. There is an obvious reason for that, which I will explain later. But for now let's say that the action we want to take is based on a combination of what feels intuitively right and what makes logical sense. Can you hear me now?"

"Huh?" I said.

"Clever. The third part of the formula is Attitude. Attitude is big. The most important aspect of attitude is how you respond to what has happened after you take action toward creating your vision. If you see positive value in whatever happens, that is the fastest way to learn what will work. The best way to approach creating anything is trial and correction. Most say 'trial and error,' but that's too negative. You try something, you learn from what happens and then you try again with new knowledge. Eventually, you are going to create your vision and learn a lot of priceless information along the way.

"One of my most gifted mentors, named Kurt, helped me see the simplicity and power of this approach. He used to say that if you work this formula, only one of two things can happen: *you will manifest the vision you were trying to bring into reality or you will get a lesson required to manifest that vision.* Simple enough?"

I nodded and smiled at her enthusiasm.

"And here's the game changer. If the only two options are either to manifest the thing you are trying to create *or* get a lesson that is required to create it, guess what else you get?" she said.

"Please tell me."

"*You can't lose!* From an objective perspective, you can only win. Do you see how powerful that is?!"

"I like it. Now I see why you're *on a roll* all of the time."

"That's actually a good answer, but I want to make sure you get the power of this formula," she said.

"I think I do. Keep talking. It probably needs to sink in."

"Do you ever have any fear about making mistakes or failing at things you try to do?"

"Sure, I have a fair amount of trepidation about my ability to do this job with you. Probably an even bigger fear is that I'm going to disappoint you."

"Exactly. So here's where the breakthrough is. What would you be like if you knew you couldn't fail?"

"That would be nice. It's a little hard to believe."

"You're already good at using this model with women. When you are trying to pick up women at the bar or at the beach, do you feel like you can fail?"

"Well, I wouldn't call it failure. I'm just trusting the process and that I know from past experience I'm going to score if I maintain my attitude and keep trying."

"That's it. You just described the formula in your own words. You are brilliant at it already."

"Well, *brilliant* might be a stretch, but I've certainly had some success."

"So here's the big question," she said.

"Hit me."

"What would you be like if you knew you couldn't fail at doing this job with me? What if you knew that somehow, no matter what, you were going to succeed?"

"I guess if I knew I was going to succeed no matter what, I would feel like a pro. I would be a pretty confident chap."

"If you embrace this formula and apply it to your new job, you are that confident chap who can't fail!"

"So what I think I hear you saying is that even though my mistakes could be potentially disastrous for the team, it's going to be a win if I learn from my mistakes and keep going."

"That's good. That's in the ballpark. I can still hear some fear of making mistakes in there," she said.

"Like I said, I'm still scared of making mistakes. I think I'm starting to get the shift. It feels like you're asking me to give up my negative judgments about how things have turned out or will turn out," I said.

"Hallelujah! I hear angels singing. Can you hear them?"

She was teasing, but I could also feel how excited she was for me.

"If you give up your negative judgments about what has just happened or what could happen, *you're on a roll, you're unstoppable.*"

"Wow, all that happens from that one little change in how you think," I said.

"You got it. I could ask, 'Can you do it' but I already know you *can* do it. The question is, *will* you do it?"

"Will I give up my negative judgments about what is happening or what I think could happen in order to be your brilliant partner whose mistakes turn out to be the reason we succeed?"

"I just had a *mental orgasm*," she said.

"Really... I'm not sure I've ever had one of those."

"Sure, you have. When you're trying to help someone get something that's really important, and then they get it in a way that you know they'll never be the same. And you helped them get it. That's one of the greatest feelings in the world. "

"First of all, I'm glad you had a mental orgasm and that I was involved somehow. I'm not sure I have totally earned such praise. My mind is fast and it gets things quickly, but that doesn't mean I have it in my experience quite yet."

"I understand. That's very perceptive, and I'm not concerned. If you can explain it back to me the way you just did, some part of you has it. The first step to any breakthrough is always new awareness. You are definitely aware in a new way."

"So now it feels like the formula is the magic, but what if I screw *that* up?" I said.

"You *will* screw it up! And that's why you'll be so good at it. I am counting on you to make mistakes and learn from them as fast as possible. That's the only way you're going to be able to keep up with me. Or, I probably should say, that's the only way you're going to be consistently at your best."

"It feels like the intensity of the game just moved up a few notches."

"You're ready, honey. I don't want you to get bored. One of the things we are good at is teaching our herd how to overcome their fears so they can do what they need to do. Most people have been programmed to be liked and not cause trouble. Getting along works fine until there's a conflict. Where we lose our power is when we ignore what we really want to do because we're afraid someone will disapprove. We've been trained to avoid conflict. In this reality, you can't create your vision without being good at dealing with conflict.

"There are always going to be adversaries who want something different or don't want what you want. You have to be good at either going around them or getting them on your team. Also, you can't let the conflicts get you down. That's the attitude part. You have to learn from whatever is happening, good or bad, and hold your vision of what you want to create.

"Another way to say it is that you have to be detached from how people respond to you. If your heart's in the right place

131

and you're doing your best, you have to learn to ignore those telling you that you've lost your mind.

"One of my favorite quotes is by Gandhi. It's so simple. He said, 'The secret to success is a burning passion and total detachment.' He was brilliant at both. He changed a major part of the world for good with a simple willingness to believe in his cause and not be deterred by the people who didn't agree with him."

"Heavy stuff," I said.

"Hey, you get me going. I can talk about this kind of thing forever. Speaking of which, I need to watch for my next meeting. The top LightSpace Project person from Japan is meeting me here at any moment. How are *we* doing?"

"Wow, it's been an hour already," I said. "Spending time with you is hypnotic. I don't know where the time goes."

"I hate to end this stimulating discussion, but I need to return a few calls before Hiro gets here. I'd love to have you meet him but he's on a tight schedule. You will meet him soon enough."

"So I have a vision, but I'm a little reluctant to share it with you."

"Oh, why is that?"

"Well, in my vision you are naked and begging me to stop."

She reached over and placed her hand on top of mine and moved in closer to me so no one could hear us. "Your assignment is to practice using the formula, and I have another request."

"What's that?"

"When we are working together, I need you to see me as a person, not as a Playboy Bunny. I realize that presents a challenge for most guys. In fact, in my experience, the smartest guys often have the strongest sex drive. So we need to keep that magical imposing protuberance of yours comfortably restrained. And in your case, I'm going to give you an extra-special incentive."

"You have my undivided attention."

"I can tell. I'm not sure I've ever had this much of your attention. I like it. So here's the deal. If you're a good boy and focus on being at your best, and see me with my clothes on, I will make the benefits beyond your imagination."

"All righty, then. I guess that covers that," I said.

"I need to get on the phone."

"Cold water comes to mind. I think I'll swim home to cool things down! My place is just at the other end of the channel. I'll wave as I swim by."

She tittered at my sexual humor and then gave me a big onetime wave with her free hand while she dialed her phone.

13. Small Minds...

The drive back to my apartment from the Ritz turned into a competition to see if I could make all the lights. I liked to test the agility of my new sports car and will admit to driving faster than I should have. But it was such intense fun.

My lunch at the Ritz was gourmet, but I didn't have time to order something sweet. A Frappuccino sounded good, so I headed for Starbucks. I was crossing Speedway, which was the street before the beach, and out of nowhere a van screeched to a stop right in front of me. Two big guys with ski masks grabbed me, handcuffed me, thrust a hood over my head, threw me in the side of the van and took off. I tried to resist and got a punch in the gut that was so hard I couldn't breathe.

I was on the floor of the van in a cargo area with my hands locked behind my back, trying to get air back in my lungs. I had moments of panic as I tried to breathe. My body screamed for air. I was furious but I felt helpless to do anything about it, which made me more angry. I suspected these were the same guys who had tossed my apartment. They had not gotten what they wanted from me yet and this was round two.

We drove around for ten minutes. They didn't say anything other than one guy told the driver where to turn a couple of times. There was a driver and the two big guys who grabbed me, as far as I could tell. I didn't know what to do. I had never been kidnapped before. I wasn't sure what they would do if I said something. I wasn't interested in getting hit again. The hood on my head said they weren't going to tell me where we were going.

The van slowed and went over a slight dip, then I heard the motor of a garage door opener. We pulled ahead and the door closed behind us. The side door of the van opened and a raspy voice said, "Come on, time to answer some questions."

"I'm not sure who you guys think I am," I said. "There must be some mistake."

"We know who you are and there's no mistake and you better shut your trap unless you want to get hit again."

"You don't need to hit me!"

He grabbed my arm behind my back and pushed it up as far as it would go. The pain was so intense I thought my arm was going to snap. "Say one more word and you'll be sucking for air."

I was careful not to say anything, although I was afraid I would scream from the pain of my twisted arm and then get hit again. They roughly bumped me along for twenty steps only to push me down onto a hard chair with no arms. The hood came off. There was a bright light so I couldn't see much. As my eyes adjusted it looked like a large empty garage with a high ceiling. The spotlight in front of me was so bright it hurt to look in that direction. One of the big guys stood a few feet away still wearing a ski mask.

"So, Mr. Lamaire, we have some questions for you." This voice came from behind the light and was younger than I expected. "If you cooperate, we'll have you on your way in no time. If we don't get the answers we want, things could get a little messy. But there's no need for that. It's totally up to you."

"I don't think I know anything, but go ahead and ask away."

"Thank you for your cooperation, Mr. Lamaire."

"You work for ASC?"

"Yes. I just started a few days ago."

"Did you have any prior contact with any of these people?"

"No, none."

"Did you know anything about this organization before you went to work for them?"

"No."

"Do you use a secret code to communicate?"

"Not that I'm aware of."

"Let me ask you that question again…do you use a secret code to communicate?"

"No, I don't know of any code."

Slaaappp! The big guy standing next to me landed a backhand across my face. I didn't feel anything at first, and then it stung like someone had pushed a bunch of needles in my face and I was seeing stars.

"Mr. Lamaire, we want to make sure you are motivated to tell us the truth."

"You don't have to hit me. I *am* telling you the truth. I have nothing to hide."

"All right, we'll come back to that. Have you met Jean Claude Chartrand?"

"Yes."

"Did you know he's a suspected arms dealer with ties to terrorist groups?"

"No, I did not know that!"

Slaaappp! I could sense that one coming but couldn't do anything about it. The delayed sting was setting in. "Why are you hitting me!?" I yelled in anger. "I met the guy one time for dinner. I don't know anything about his business."

"What did you discuss at dinner?"

"He is one of the founders of ASC. They want me to do sales and sales training. That's what we talked about."

"Mr. Lamaire, we're going to let you think about this for a few days. We don't think you're telling us everything. Maybe your memory will improve after a little more encouragement from Mr. Smith and Mr. Jones. They will be checking in on you from time to time to give you some additional incentives to tell us what we want to know."

"You can't hold me here. I haven't broken any laws. Plus, I don't know anything. I just started with the company. Who *are* you people?"

"Maybe after you've had some time to think about our questions, you will be able to remember more. You've been seen with suspected terrorists, Mr. Lamaire. We have to do what we can to protect our country."

"I don't know anything. I'm the new guy. I haven't been with the company long enough to know anything. I'm not going to know any more tomorrow! What do you think I'm going to know tomorrow that I don't know now!?"

"I guess we'll have to wait to find out," said Mr. Jones.

"Unbelievable," I said.

Slaaappp! Mr. Jones backhanded me across the face one more time.

"We don't want your opinion," said Mr. Jones with his raspy voice. "You don't speak unless we tell you to."

Then he put a piece of duct tape over my mouth and taped my ankles to the legs of the chair. I wanted to tell the guy to go to hell as the sting and the pain of the slap intensified. I couldn't respond now anyway. Within a few minutes everyone seemed to be gone. I couldn't hear anyone. They left me in the room with the light on. There were no windows and one door, as far as I could see.

They said I was going to be there for days and they sounded confident they could do whatever they wanted with me. Basically, I had no rights. They can't leave me like this. I can't go to the bathroom. Or maybe that's part of the torture, to make me hold it until I can't anymore and suffer the inevitable.

Whatever happened, I had to look at this as a test. I needed to start thinking like a lightspace candidate. The first thing was to maintain a positive vision of the future. If I allowed myself to become afraid for my life or to be negative in any way, I reduced my chances of getting out of this. I had to stay in a mindset that allowed me to be as resourceful as possible at all times. If I missed one little thing, that could be the difference between living and dying.

So my goal, my vision, was to get out of there as fast as possible, and preferably without further injury. The next question was, what action could I take? What did I know to do? What felt intuitively right?

The logical answer was to try to get out of the handcuffs. But I should also be asking my intuition what was the smartest thing to do at this point. I had to calm myself down like in a meditation and wait for an answer rather than try to figure it out.

No one was bothering me at this point, so I relaxed and got into a more quiet state. After a couple minutes, the thought that came to me was a vision of Sophia. We were connected on a psychic level—I knew it. I needed to let her know I was in trouble. Maybe she could figure out a way to find me. So I focused my thoughts and imagined sending a message to Sophia. I imagined her getting the message and knowing what to do. I sent my psychic message to her over and over, *Sophia, I'm in trouble. I need help.* After a few minutes, I realized that if she was going to get my message, she had gotten it by now. I decided to see what else I could do to better my situation.

There wasn't much I could do other than be calm and not worry myself with all the negative things that could happen to me. Sophia and I had talked about how destructive worrying was and that it didn't contribute anything positive to your situation. In fact, it made it worse. So rather than worrying about the negatives, which most people would find totally justified in this situation, I decided to go with my instincts again.

I was going to act as if I was going to get out of this somehow, and I didn't need to know how. Trusting that a solution would present itself felt like a better approach than working myself into a state of panic. I didn't know the first thing about getting out of handcuffs, so why pretend? I was relatively comfortable, other than my face hurt from being slapped by the biggest of the three stooges.

My watch wasn't visible, but my guess was an hour had passed. I could hear voices and then the door opened. It was the two big guys that had grabbed me. That was a good sign. The younger thug was not with them, or I hoped he wasn't. If he weren't there, it was not as likely they would try that hard to get more information out of me. But that didn't mean they wouldn't knock me around for the fun of it.

"So you ready to talk yet?" said the raspy voice as he ripped the duct tape off my mouth.

I let the sting of the duct tape wear off before I spoke. I could only see his eyes through the ski mask. "Like I told you guys before, I wish I knew something I could tell you so you'd let me go. But I don't know anything."

"Maybe we should pull out a few of your teeth and see if that helps you remember anything." He snickered as if he had done that before and liked it. "Or maybe we cut off a couple of your fingers. That usually helps. Doesn't it, Mr. Smith?"

"Yep, I've seen idiots like you get really smart when we start cutting off parts of your body. It's amazing what you can remember. There's one part that good-looking guys like you really hate to lose. You know which part I mean, Mr. Jones?"

"I do, Mr. Smith. It would be a shame for this dickhead to become one of them *uniques* just because he couldn't remember something. Although I hear they can get a job guarding a whorehouse. They're not afraid you'll be trying to sample the merchandise, if you know what I mean." They both laughed like monsters in a horror movie. That was harder to ignore.

"But you're in luck," said Jones. "We're going to let you sleep on it tonight. Maybe sitting in that chair all night will help you remember things. And you don't need to worry if you have to take a shit. Just hold it. That way we can beat the crap out of you when we come back. We'll get our morning workout by using you as a punching bag before we start cutting off body parts. So have a pleasant evening, Luke. Or should we call you *Louise*?"

As Mr. Jones finished his sentence accompanied by his demonic laugh, there was a zipping sound that flashed across the room. Something had hit Mr. Jones in the chest. Mr. Smith's eyes mushroomed as he watched Mr. Jones crumple to the ground. He turned to see where the noise had come from, the zipping sound happened again, and now Mr. Smith was slowly falling to the ground. I had never heard that sound except on TV but I recognized it instantly—it was a gun with a silencer. The shots came from behind the light so I couldn't see the shooter. To my surprise and delight, Mr. Smith and Mr. Jones were not so talkative anymore. They were both in a pile on the floor.

"Luke," said a new voice that also sounded familiar.

"Yes, I'm Luke. I hope you're here to save me from the evil twins."

"Luke, it's Diego. Let me get you out of that chair."

"Diego, man, am I glad to see you! I had a suspicion you might be a multipurpose chauffeur. Nice shooting. Are they dead?"

"No, we try not to kill anyone. But they are out cold."

"You saved me from a fate worse than death. There was a third guy. Did you get him?"

"Not this go-around. But these guys won't bother you again. Their memories will be erased to where they'll barely remember their names. They won't remember anything about you or Sophia or Jean Claude. And their buddies will think twice about giving you a hard time knowing they could end up the same way."

"Who are those guys?"

"Military dropouts hired by Homeland Security."

"Really?" I said. "Those guys didn't make it past eighth grade."

"They're sloppy hires to fill some government quota. They are *way* too enthusiastic about torturing innocent citizens in the name of patriotism. Having to deal with these types is an occupational hazard for you, I'm afraid."

"I owe you my life."

"You don't owe me anything. Just doing my job. Now you go and do yours. We're counting on you to kick ass at what you do."

"I promise to do my best." That was a surprise. Diego of all people. The man of few words turns out to be a super-spy and probably knows the secrets of all the players.

"There you go," said Diego, as he finished getting me free. Finally, I could move again. "There are two guys waiting for you in a black Escalade to the right outside the door. The passphrase is 'Did you go to Pepperdine?' *They* will ask you the question. If they don't give you the passphrase right away, run in the other direction as fast as you can, and I will take care of it. Better get out of here before anyone else shows up. I will deal with these deviates."

"Thanks again, Diego. Like I said, I owe you big-time."

"Don't give it another thought, really. Remember, you never saw me and this didn't happen."

"Got it." So that's how it works. This never happened and Mr. Smith and Mr. Jones will wake up tomorrow with amnesia and start new lives.

"You better get moving," said Diego.

I quickly found my getaway ride and within twenty minutes was having my favorite cocktail on my new leather couch.

Even with the crap scared out of me, I felt safer. I felt more important and more protected than before. Diego's comment that getting grabbed and beaten up was an occupational hazard was not comforting. At least, I now knew there were reinforcements.

The LightSpace Project was much more real to me after being kidnapped. Sophia and Jean Claude had enemies that I needed to better understand. And the hombre who had just saved my life by neutralizing everyone in my immediate vicinity said he was counting on me to kick ass.

Why did they pick *me* to join the lightspace team? Maybe I really did have an important role to play. Maybe the more evolved version of me knew all about this and the current version of me had some catching up to do. The catching-up part sounded right. I had another shot of Herradura.

14. Meditative Power...

There was knock on my door. "Anyone home?" said my favorite voice in the world.

"Sophia, come in. Man, am I glad to see you!" I gave her a big hug and got one back. "Come in and sit down on my new couch."

"Nice couch. I heard you got a chance to meet one of our enemies."

"There's more than one?" I sat down next to her on the couch.

"Unfortunately, not everyone likes us. How are you doing? You look okay. Did they hurt you?"

"I got slapped hard a few times, but I'm all right. They were talking about pulling my teeth out and cutting off body parts, so I'm glad I didn't have to stay for that."

"I didn't think the bad guys were going to be that interested in you, but maybe I have to rethink that. They're coming after you pretty hard for a new guy. You don't know anything that would be of any real value but you are an easier target. We will make some adjustments to protect you better."

"What does that involve?"

"Don't be concerned about that right now. The good news is that you're not hurt. And, I'm interested in what your thought process was during your capture."

"I tried to be a good lightspace candidate and follow the formula. Keeping a positive vision and not worrying about what could happen to me was the hardest. There were a few times I could have panicked and been an emotional basket case, but I blocked out the negatives and tried to work the problem."

"I'm proud of you. That's impressive that you were able to do that with so little training. What was your vision?"

"To trust there would be a way out if I paid attention and didn't lose my focus."

"Excellent."

"I was surprised at how angry I got at being put in handcuffs and being slapped around by gorillas. Keeping my mouth shut was harder than I thought it would be, even after they hit me so hard it knocked the wind out of me."

"So how do you feel about this job now that you know it can get a little rough?"

"That's putting it mildly. You mean like losing body parts and being beaten to death?"

"Yes, those situations are not off the table yet."

"They will be off the table at some point, right?"

"Yes. When you reach lightspace, you are protected from that sort of thing."

"I don't suppose you can tell me how that works?"

"Not yet. Be patient, you'll get there."

"And, is it possible to give me a little more protection until I get there?"

"Yes, I will see to that myself. I don't want anything to happen to you. You are too important to me."

"So what do we do now? I feel like celebrating! How about you?" I said.

"I can understand why you would want to get really hammered right now, but that probably isn't the best thing to do."

"Really? Why do you say that?"

"Going unconscious after a traumatic experience isn't usually a good idea. It is what most people do, but you and I are not most people. It's better to work on something constructive and be aware of any feelings that are coming through from the ordeal. There is a part of you that's in a state of shock and needs to process what happened. If you drink a lot now, you are burying your feelings and they will come back to bite you. Plus you'll be hungover and we don't have time for that."

"I want to spend time with *you* if that's possible. I'd rather party but if that's not an option, I can adjust," I said reluctantly.

"I know you can. Let's spend some time together and see what we can accomplish and then we can take a break. But let's keep the drugs and stimulants to a minimum during break time, agreed?"

"I hate to say it, but you're probably right."

"You ready to get to work?" she said.

"Really, right now?" I got the *you're going to have to keep up* look. "Okay boss, what's next?"

"Let's talk about meditation," she said. "The way I was taught to achieve lightspace, meditation plays an important role. You said you meditate now, right?"

"Yes, almost every day."

"For how long?"

"Twenty minutes, sometimes longer."

"Has it helped you?"

"Big-time. I'm a different person because of meditation. Much more peaceful, much more intuitive, much less judgmental and there are many more miracles in my life than when I didn't meditate."

"That's the idea, all right," she said. "How did you get interested in meditation? Most Americans who try to meditate give up after a few attempts because there is not enough happening. We are too accustomed to using our conscious mind for everything. We can't understand how sitting and doing nothing is going to help us."

"I never paid any attention to meditation until I started hanging out with monks at the Monastery in Long Beach. As an aspirant, I was taught to meditate at least twice a day for fifteen minutes. The monks did a lot more. Then a few years later, I enrolled in a course from Self-Realization Fellowship which helped me get into it even more."

"I've heard of them," she said. "Aren't they here in L.A.?"

"Yes. There are SRF meditation centers all over the world, but Yogananda, the founder, actually lived here in Southern California most of his adult life. He is my favorite spiritual author. We studied him extensively when I was active in the Monastery. Have you ever been to the Lake Shrine Temple in Pacific Palisades?"

"No, but I've heard it's beautiful and I would like to go with you sometime. Are there women priests there?"

"Oh yeah. Women play a big role. Yogananda's predecessor was a woman when he transitioned in the early 1950s, and the current leader is a woman as well."

"I like women leaders," she said.

"Me too."

"Why do you meditate?"

"I'm more easygoing. I'm happier. I'm easier to be around. Little things don't bother me as much. Better attitude in general. I'm better under pressure. I'm better at taking risks and knowing the right risks to take. I make fewer mistakes. I'm more accepting, more compassionate, more understanding, more patient, more kind, more loving. How's that?"

"That's really good. I am going to put you in charge of promoting meditation to our people. Have you ever had to explain meditation to anyone?"

"Sure, my coaching clients ask me if I meditate, and we get into the discussion from there."

"What do you say to them?" she asked.

"Meditation is about focusing your conscious mind on something other than your thoughts. It doesn't mean to get rid of your thoughts exactly. But when you get your conscious mind busy doing something relatively easy, you can hear another voice that is much more subtle and harder to hear."

"Do you actually hear a voice?"

"I don't know what else to call it. Sometimes I think I hear a voice. Other times it can be a thought or a feeling. It's different somehow. It has a special quality that is hard to describe."

"I know what you mean," she said.

"Often the information comes to me as I write things down."

"You write during your meditation?"

"Some of my best insights have come from writing down what I get when I'm meditating. Then when I'm done writing, I close my eyes and go back to my internal focus."

"One of the most important benefits of meditation is access to higher intelligence," she said. "People call it different things like the subconscious, or your intuitive mind, or God or the Universe. I don't think it matters what you call it. The important thing is that it works and anyone can do it. Were you able to stay relatively calm when you were kidnapped?"

"At first I was really angry and wanted to fight back and couldn't think of anything else. Then I had the thought that I needed to be as resourceful as possible to put the odds in my favor. That's when I calmed myself and started to ask better questions. Then it occurred to me to send you a message to say I was in trouble and see if you could find me. How did you find me, by the way? I forgot all about that," I said.

147

"We had a couple of options. As it turned out, the bad guys were sloppy. They put your cell phone and your wallet in a bag and ignored it. Most important, they left your cell phone on. We have access to resources that can track your cell phone, so we were lucky this time."

"What was the other option?"

"You have not been approved to know the other option yet. Let's just say it's top secret and involves some unusual resources."

"Sounds pretty mysterious." I smiled to let her know I was good with not knowing the details and ready to move on.

"So do you see that your ability to get into a meditative state may have saved your life?"

"I guess you're right. I had never considered that perspective but I get it. Meditation saved my life. Wow, that's a new story to tell."

"That is an important story and you're going to get to share it."

I cherished her praise and enjoyed the moment.

"Let's take this conversation in another direction. Have you ever been driving home after work or cleaning up after cooking a meal and had a major insight on something?"

"Sure, that has happened many times," I said.

"That's what happens for me when I meditate," she said. "I get really quiet with a simple focus, and answers to my questions start to come to me. It's quite remarkable."

"So you ask yourself questions?" I said.

"Yeah, like you mentioned the other day that you like to ask your intuition questions and then you get answers at some point. It's the same when I meditate. I ask myself questions and wait for the answers. You never know when you're going to get your answers, and often they show up when you least expect them. Although I have asked a question and gotten an answer in the same meditation. You just have to be patient and let it come to you and not give up if you don't get an answer right away."

"Come to think of it, I have done that and it works really well. People I respect say to meditate on the problem and you will get an answer from a higher source."

"Being in a meditative state is actually a quality of lightspace. The difference is that you stay in that higher space all the time. You can learn to function in the normal world and keep your meditative high," she said.

"I've heard the advanced monks in the Monastery talk about it that same way. They say you can keep a meditative high as long as you want."

"That's right. There are a lot of advanced spiritual seekers who have achieved lightspace. They may not call it lightspace, but it's similar. They have developed the ability to stay in the higher vibration. That group will help us when the time comes. They will play an important role. Our challenge is to get more regular folks like you and me to achieve lightspace…a lot more."

"I would love to know who is making these decisions," I said.

"Someday you will. It wouldn't change anything if you *did* know. You just have to trust that the challenge is real and failure this time is final. We don't get another chance to try again like we have for thousands of years. We are so accustomed to having unlimited time and another chance to fail that we see the failure to evolve as no big deal."

"So what's the key to success, coach?" I asked.

"We have to find human beings who are aware enough of their spirit to *want* to make the leap. People like you. Most are too far into their old habits and ways of thinking to make the shift. But we only need 10 percent and we have about 1 percent now."

"One percent of the population has achieved lightspace already? How did they do it?"

"Many of them are monks, nuns, a few priests, highly developed martial artists, a few accomplished athletes, some highly creative types like performers, artists, writers and a bunch of personal growth junkies like yourself. It could be anybody really. Some people hear the call and somehow find their path. There are lots of ways to reach lightspace if you are disciplined and get the right help along the way. Following your intuitive instincts and finding the positive in whatever happens to you is a big part of it."

"And you said these people will help us?"

"Yes, but we aren't ready for them yet. We have work to do. There needs to be a structure to hold the lightspacers. We need to connect them and encourage them. And we need to find the other 9 percent!"

"So do you have a plan, Your Highness? Do you have a vision?"

"Let's walk and I will share a couple of my ideas," she said. "And please don't call me 'Your Highness'!"

"Sorry. You're right, that was weird energy. Thanks for putting up with me. I'm more upset about everything that happened to me than I realize."

To say I wasn't scared to walk past the place where Mr. Smith and Mr. Jones grabbed me would be an understatement. Sophia assured me that we were safe for reasons she didn't want to get into. I believed her but I was more scared than I thought I would be. I could see what she meant now about the importance of letting the feelings come through from being abducted or they would haunt me. She was smart to get me right back on the horse that threw me and get me to walk to the beach. It was a favorite thing to do. It was one of the reasons I lived in L.A. I couldn't let the bad guys keep me from walking on the beach or walking anywhere I wanted to go, for that matter.

Sophia let me babble on about being abducted. She listened but didn't seem too concerned. She was letting me vent and process as I relived the experience of being kidnapped.

"When you experience things more completely," she said, "you tend to let them go. They disappear from your awareness. It's the things you have avoided experiencing, like things you're afraid of or things you're in denial about, that are the biggest problem.

"One of my mentors said it's like leaving a steel rake in the yard with the teeth up. You don't see the rake until you step on the teeth, and then the handle smacks you in the chin. If you don't put the rake away, it's just a matter of time before you step on the rake again and it smacks you in the chin one more time. It's the same with unresolved issues and unexperienced events. Until we allow ourselves to feel what really happened to us, we will avoid anything that looks remotely like the thing we're afraid of. Can you see how that would be a hazard in this job?"

"Sure, I don't want to be avoiding anything out of fear of an unresolved past experience. It will keep me from being objective and resourceful."

"Exactly. To be at our best, we need to be as fearless as possible, and that takes work. You can do some of the debrief with me because we are together a lot. But it's also good to have a relationship just for that purpose with someone like Angela who is trained to do that kind of listening.

"Our relationship will be more productive if we focus on what we are trying to create together and let a designated coach deal with any baggage that shows up. You and I want to use our energy to get as much work done as we can and enjoy our time together when we take breaks. Does that make sense?"

"Yes, it does, and I also know there will be things that I will only want to discuss with you. Is that all right?" I asked.

"Of course. If something comes up that is bothering you, run it by me so I can decide if I want to address it or defer it."

"Sounds like a plan. I feel lucky to have a boss who's so smart. Most of the bosses I've had turned out to be pretty limited in their scope. I felt like I could do my job and their job better than they could within a short amount of time."

"There's an important difference between them and me. I would be thrilled if you can do your job *and* my job better than I can. If you and I can harness all that intelligence and put it into action, we will make history."

"I guess that's our challenge, to make sure there *are* history books and, most important, humans around to read them."

"Right on." She raised her clenched fist in the air. "I have one more question about how you meditate."

"Sure."

"What do you do to start your meditation?"

"I thank God and the Great Spirit for my life and all my gifts and blessings. I acknowledge that I have to go halfway to them. They can't come all the way to me. I ask that I be helped to see my Higher Intelligence so I can make the greatest contribution to the people's lives I touch. I give thanks for the miracles that have been sent to me and the protection I have been given. Things like that. I don't always do the same thing. I change it up when I hear something new that I like."

"That's beautiful. I'm particularly interested in the *protection* part. Do you feel like you have been protected?"

"Lots of times. Sometimes more than I probably deserve."

"Why do you say that?" she asked.

"I've done my share of stupid things in life that could have gotten me in big trouble and been devastating for others as well. Sometimes I feel like I have an obligation to serve and do my best because I've been spared a disastrous fate more than once. Someone is definitely watching out for me."

"It's good that you see you've had protections. Your experience of being protected is going to get much stronger as you get closer to lightspace. The protection at that level is more powerful than you can imagine. You will feel the ability to take much greater risks."

"I read Yogananda's interpretation of the *Bhagavad Gita* when I was active in the Monastery. In that piece was one of the most moving things I have ever read. Krishna, which I learned means 'Christ' in Hindu, was talking to Arjuna, who was his disciple at that time some 5,000 years ago."

"I'm familiar with the *Gita*. It's one of the most profound descriptions of the challenge we face to get to lightspace. So what did Krishna say?"

"'Keep *your focus on me and all your needs will be met and your gains made permanent.*' When I heard that for the first time, the impact of that simple phrase shot from my brain to my toes in an instant. I could feel the truth in my heart. From that moment on I was committed to the search for my spirit and my connection to my Higher Self."

"Thank you for sharing that with me. You say the most amazing things."

Being acknowledged by Sophia was becoming one of my favorite experiences in life. I gazed back at her with great love and appreciation.

When we got back to my apartment, Sophia mentioned there was more royalty in town and she needed to get ready for a dinner party. She wanted me to take the night off and get some quiet time. That sounded good to me. She also asked me to come up with some ideas on how to speed up the process of helping people go from separated egos to intuitive spirits. She said we needed a breakthrough in that department to keep the bosses happy. I said I would give it some *mind time*, which was my process of meditating on a subject and seeing what insights and answers appeared. It was like asking the Universe to tell us what to do next. That would be a good assignment for me.

We said our goodbyes, being especially thankful that our new partnership would live to see another day. I got a hug and a kiss that made me feel like a king.

15. Headed for NYC...

Sophia was a superior recruiter. Her ability to hire the right people had caused our little LightSpace Project to take on a life of its own. Hundreds of the most highly developed seekers from all over the world were asking how they could help with whatever was needed.

Since we had advocates everywhere, the Internet was going to be a key element. We needed a way to offer training and support. We wanted all of our tribe to be in communication with each other. They would help us find and train more candidates. One of Sophia's goals was to have a satellite office in every time zone around the world as soon as possible.

Teleconference calls and webinars were happening every day, many hosted by Sophia. One of her many gifts was her presence and charisma in front of a room or on a conference call with hundreds of participants. There was the constant training of new hires to host more calls and webinars on many subjects. We needed armies of skilled coaches and trainers. We needed good interpreters. We needed to find financial resources. And here's the kicker, it was the most magical thing I had ever seen. Whatever we needed in terms of people or resources just seemed to appear within days of asking for it.

I had originally thought finding and training our members would be more difficult and tedious. I thought back to when I first heard the preposterous notion that a group of intelligent beings from other planets had decided that Earth had one more chance to prove it could be peaceful before they turned out the lights and called it a failed experiment. I was not relishing the idea of having the same conversations that Sophia had to have with me to get me on the team. I had overlooked that those who were attracted to our mission were highly intuitive. They instantly knew if what we were saying was true or not.

Like seeing fire for the first time, once you knew it was real, it wasn't so outrageous anymore. You made whatever paradigm adjustments you needed to make and it quickly became a new truth about the reality of life. The outrageous new reality that our days were numbered unless we made some difficult choices created an opening for change and growth that had never existed before.

There was a multitude of bright spirits out there just waiting for something big to happen, and they all wanted to be part of a new direction. Sure, they had a gazillion questions, but the lack of details didn't create the usual doubt and fear. They were not calling us lunatics or liars. They could see who we were and that what we were up to was a good thing. They wanted to know how they could be involved!

Sophia had spent hours with me on the enrollment process, which was one of her many strengths. She had an uncanny ability to ask the right question at the right time. I was getting a better feel for knowing where these conversations needed to go and how to ask the right questions. There were so many new people to talk to both in person and on the phone, it was more fun than work. Of course, I thought anyone interested in our project was quite extraordinary. The more people we talked to, the faster the word was spreading on its own. So really everyone we were talking to was more than interested, which made the interviews easy. The number of beings moving toward us was overwhelming at times, but that was a challenge we welcomed.

Senior staff decided that I would fly to New York to meet with green-energy billionaire Lon Prince. He was the brother of Lila Prince, a recent recruit from Seattle. Lila said her brother was a personal growth dynamo who had done many popular programs. He had gotten to a leadership level with Landmark Education, which was a key element in my own evolution. Having that philosophy in common would jumpstart our relationship. It also meant a great deal to me that Sophia endorsed the *Landmark Forum* as one of the best trainings for giving people a glimpse of who they really are *and* who they can be.

Everyone was excited for me and convinced I would do well in the Big Apple. I had talked with close to a hundred aspirants in the last two weeks, many highly positioned candidates, but the interview with Lon seemed like a bigger deal somehow. I was getting good at the enrollment conversation. The added pressure was to acquire more funding sources. Our LightSpace Project was growing at an exponential rate and we were going to need more financial resources to keep up with the pace of our expansion. This was anticipated by the founders and was part of the business plan. I had a feeling that finding financial resources might become a part of my job description. I enjoyed the enrollment process with new recruits, but there was a different kind of juice that came from promotion. I loved to promote things I believed in and get others to support the cause by writing a check.

Diego gave me a ride to LAX. Waiting to board the plane gave me time to wind down and listen to some music. Candy had put me on a nonstop Economy flight with a window seat in the fourth row with extra legroom. That arrangement was actually quite comfortable. There was no First Class seating on this flight so this was the next best thing. There was no one sitting next to me, and a white-haired grandma type with her knitting needles sat in the aisle seat. Otherwise, the cabin was about 80 percent full.

So, what to do for the next four hours? I had brought my MacAir laptop, which was one of my favorite things in the world, and there was Internet access on the plane. I had some research to do for my meeting with Lon Prince but I wasn't ready for that. A glass of wine would be nice, but that usually led to several glasses and then I would sleep the last two hours of the flight. Somehow, that didn't sound like as much fun as usual. I decided to work on my bucket list. There were a couple of items I needed to add. I really wanted to do well at my new job. Having the world end would make my bucket list rather irrelevant and that didn't feel right. Also, making love to Sophia for hours at a time was an obvious addition that got a circle and an exclamation point.

Then I tried to determine if anything else felt like its time had come. I was often pleasantly surprised at my discoveries. I was not trying to figure out what would make sense for me to do next. I was waiting for something on the list to call to me. I finally decided to meditate on the view from my window seat and wait for the inspiration of whatever I was supposed to do next.

The first hour of the flight out of L.A. was so spectacular, with the mountains, the valleys, the lakes, the riverbeds, the occasional wisp of smoke from a forest fire and the majestic cumulus clouds glowing in the afternoon sun. The experience of looking at Earth from 30,000 feet and the pure rush of how far you could see was a never-ending source of awe. I cranked up my playlist of female jazz vocalists with a four-octave range and just took it all in.

Sophia had been busier than ever, which had not given us much time to hang out. We were stealing time for a meal here and there, but work was always part of the conversation.

My job was becoming almost as fast and furious as hers. Even though we were seeing less of each other, my feelings for her had grown stronger. There were more hot, intelligent women walking in and out of the ASC office than ever, but there was only one Sophia. My attraction to her was way more than physical at this point, which was usually how these things got started. There was a whole combination of things I got from being in her presence—energy, love, companionship, confidence, intelligence. Whatever it was, it was addictive in ways I had never felt or imagined before.

We both knew what we'd signed up for. We knew with the stakes so high our jobs would become all-consuming. Our hope was that there would be more time for us at some point down the road. In the meantime, we would support each other to be at our best and try to find some time to be together. The bigger looming reality was that if we didn't do our jobs well, there might not be a world to hang out in. Being in love with Sophia was something I would have to wait to fully express, which was the hardest thing I ever had to do.

We were three hours into a smooth flight when I heard a loud thud by the front entrance where the stews hang out. Then I saw a flight attendant fly across the aisle and crash into the side of the plane as if she were thrown by a gorilla. Then two flight attendants appeared from their forward station and walked by me headed for the back of the plane. The first one looked scared and upset, like she was about to burst into tears. She was the one who had been manhandled. The second one had no expression, like she was trying to do everything she could to not feel anything.

A voice came on the loudspeaker. "My name is Amir, and I am taking command of the airplane. I have a gun. Do what I say or you will be shot."

There was an instant expression of terror, then total silence. Then a woman toward the back of the cabin burst into tears. You could hear the person next to her telling her to stop crying or she could be the first to die. That made her cry even louder for a few seconds, and then she stopped crying but continued to have trouble breathing, which everyone on the plane could hear.

Then Amir appeared from behind the flight attendant area. He was about six feet tall, athletic build, dressed in a black suit, white dress shirt and patterned brown tie. He then slowly took off his tie and put it in his pocket as he studied the people on the plane. He seemed to want to let us know this wasn't his first rodeo. He had a .50-caliber Dezzy in his other hand the whole time. I wondered how he got such a big gun on the plane. Clean-shaven, short dark hair, late twenties—he looked like a regular young businessman in a suit. Not what you'd expect for a terrorist. Except he had penetrating cold eyes and an expressionless, dead face. This guy was the real deal.

"You people in the first three rows, get up and go find a seat in the back of the plane. Hurry, do it now!" he yelled in a commanding voice.

Everyone was scared and fumbling around, grabbing their stuff. Amir looked irritated. Then an older woman started to complain.

"Young man, I'm sorry but I have an oxygen tank and I need a seat with extra room for my tank. If I move to the back of the plane I won't have room for my oxygen tank."

There was a blast that was so loud your ears went numb. He had shot the complaining woman in the forehead. The resultant blood spatter covered the side of the plane from floor to ceiling. The remaining passengers from the first three rows sprinted to empty seats. Another older woman tripped and fell in the aisle. Two horrified passengers stepped on her to get to a seat as fast as possible. Then the woman on the floor became hysterical, crying and pleading, "Don't kill me! Don't kill me! I can't walk!"

Amir barked, "Help that woman get to a seat or I will kill her!"

Several of the guys jumped to the woman's aid and got her to a seat. I made a mental note of the three men who jumped up to help the woman, although it was hard to tell if they were being brave or reacting out of fear.

I was now in the front row of people in the cabin and closest to our captor. That could prove useful. Everyone back at the office said I was the one they wanted to send to meet billionaire Lon Prince. Sophia had said she had a good feeling about this trip. Who knew I would be on a hijacked airplane trying to figure out how to subdue a terrorist? I needed to use my training. Be objective and work the problem. No time for emotions. No fear, no doubt, just the confidence that my Higher Self would lead me to the best possible course of action. I had to focus on my highest intuitive awareness.

We had no indication of what Amir was planning. He didn't seem to be in any hurry to let us know. But I had no idea how long that would last. We were 60 minutes out from landing at JFK. I needed to mobilize a strike team to overcome Amir. We could use our cell phones so we could text without being noticed. So far, Amir seemed to be working alone, so I could try passing a note without being exposed by a confederate. I wrote on the outside of the note, *Pass back to stewardess.* Inside I wrote, *Text this number to stop Amir: 303-202-1155.*

I turned off the tones and left Vibrate on. My hope was that we could find a group of guys in the cabin who would rush Amir if I could somehow distract him or tackle him. They would have to be able to get to the front of the cabin fast. We would only have a couple of seconds. Amir had already demonstrated he was physically strong and a *shoot first, ask questions later* kind of guy.

How was I going to approach him? I could try to get him into a conversation about something he wanted to talk about, like his cause and his hate for the West. Much would depend on what Amir was planning for us, which I knew would be challenging. He was a coldhearted killer.

I got a text. That didn't take long. The text said, *What do we do?*

I texted back, *Is there air marshal or similar on board?*

No.

Can you group text?

I think so.

Do you have passenger list and cell numbers?

Not all but most.

Start texting the men. Ask if they can fight. Will they rush Amir on my command? Put yeses together for a group text and send seat numbers.

What if I get caught?

You won't. Be discreet.

What's your name? Where are you?

Don't use real name or location. I'm Batman, toward front. How about you?

Robin. You know where I am.

Get to work Robin. We can take this plane back.

Roger that.

Amir was fumbling with the microphone, getting ready to use the intercom. "This is Amir again. This intercom can be heard by everyone on the plane, including the pilots. So listen carefully. I have a high-tech altimeter and compass. I know if the plane changes course or altitude. If we stay on our current course for JFK at our current altitude, there will not be a problem. If I get an indication that the plane has changed course or altitude, I will shoot a passenger every 30 seconds until the plane reaches its original course and altitude. Is that understood? Pilots, I need to know that you understand what I have just said. Please respond or I will kill another passenger."

"We understand!" yelled one of the pilots, obviously upset.

"Very good. Also, no one is to leave their seat for any reason. If I see anyone standing in the aisle, I will shoot you, and I am a very good shot. Is that understood?"

There was a garbled response from people saying yes and others just making a sound because they were too scared to talk.

"If someone has to use the bathroom, I will allow one person at a time to go to the back of the plane. If I see two of

161

you standing at the same time, I will shoot you both. Is that clear? Flight attendants, raise your hands. Okay. The flight attendant closest to the bathroom is in charge of getting people to the bathroom and then back to their seat one at a time. What is your name?"

"Stephanie."

"Stephanie, you're in charge. Do it quietly or someone will be shot. I will be back in a few minutes. In the meantime, I encourage you to call your friends and family and let them know you are on a hijacked airplane and someone has already been killed. You can take videos and pictures and put them on the Internet, but stay seated and do this quietly. If anyone gets too loud, you will be shot. Also—and this is very important— no talking to anyone else on the plane. You can make calls on your cell but otherwise no talking to your neighbor or anyone else on the plane, and this includes flight attendants. If I see anyone talking to each other, I will shoot you both. I don't want to talk to anyone and I don't want to answer any questions. Do what I ask, and you won't be shot."

The plane had been hijacked by the easily irritated, trigger-happy Amir, who appeared to be a fearless smart guy with nothing to lose, the worst kind of adversary. I dialed Sophia to see if I could get her involved.

"Luke, what a pleasant surprise. Is everything all right?"

"Actually, no. The plane has been hijacked by a guy named Amir."

"How close are you to landing?"

"About an hour out. No idea what he's up to yet, except he has already shot a woman in the forehead for complaining with a very large handgun."

"He is letting you use your cell phones?"

"Yes. He is encouraging people to call their loved ones and to take pictures and videos and put them on the Internet."

"Can you communicate with the flight attendants?"

"Already did that. She has a list of cell numbers and is identifying guys who would be willing to rush Amir. Her code

162

name is Robin. I'm Batman. I am emailing you her number from my computer. She probably has a protocol she has to follow but you could offer your help."

"Any air marshal?"

"No."

"Let me find out if she'll let me help her. Be back to ya."

16. Two Sides...

Fifteen minutes had passed since Amir had addressed the cabin and the pilots. He was in no hurry to make demands or even tell us what he was planning to do. You could hear people quietly chattering away, calling everyone they knew and telling them what was happening. I had checked the Internet to see if we were being covered by the news. They were all over it. Passengers were taking pictures and videos and sending them to news outlets. Part of Amir's plan was becoming obvious.

I got a call from Robin to let me know there were three guys who would be willing to rush the front of the plane if I could distract Amir. There were several others who were willing to help but said they were scared they would not be fast enough or strong enough. One of the fighters was only three rows back from me, the other two were more than ten rows back. I told Robin to have the top three guys text me so I could communicate with them. She then told me that Sophia and her team were helping her create the group texts and communicating with passengers to determine who would be the best three men to lead the charge with Batman. I confirmed that Sophia was the smartest person I had ever met and would be a crucial resource. Robin said she had to report to the air marshal's office, but they were encouraging her to use whatever assets were available.

Amir was fumbling with the microphone.

"Okay, everyone. It looks like we've gotten the attention of the major news networks. So now I'm going to interview some of you and talk about why I have taken over this plane. I encourage some of you to video these conversations and get them on the Internet. Let's start with you in the aisle seat in row 7. Start with your name, how old you are and what you do for a living."

"Do you want me to stand?" said the man.

"No, stay seated. I can hear you."

"My name is Harold Deacon. I'm 53 and I own my own business."

"What kind of business do you own, Harold?" Amir looked irritated again.

"We sell security systems for commercial buildings."

"Security systems. So you're trying to keep the bad guys from breaking in and stealing stuff."

"Sure, that's one way to put it."

"You are correct, that is one way to put it. Harold Deacon, do I have that right?"

"Yes, that is my name."

"Okay, Harold. Do you think I'm a bad guy?"

"I am a little concerned that if I don't answer the question right, you will shoot me."

"That is correct, Harold. That could happen. So let me ask you again. Do you think I am one of the bad guys?"

"I'm afraid to say anything. You shot that poor woman for complaining."

"Harold, if you don't answer my question, I *will* shoot you."

"All right, well, you've taken over an airplane by force and you've already killed someone. Most people would have trouble calling that being one of the—" BAM! A thunderous blast tore through the cabin.

Amir had pointed his gun at Harold Deacon and pulled the trigger. He had hardly aimed and hit him dead center in the middle of his forehead from twenty feet. Harold was now slumped over with his chin on his chest and blood running down his face. Some of the blood from the exit wound had sprayed over the back of his seat onto the passengers sitting behind him. The cabin was dead quiet. Amir was going to be more dangerous to overtake than I had previously thought. He was unconsciously good with that gun.

"So let that be a lesson to everyone," Amir said in a quiet voice like nothing had happened. "I want straight and direct answers. I gave Harold three chances to answer a *yes or no* question and he couldn't do it. So let's try someone else. You in the plaid shirt. Yeah, you. What's your name, your age and what do you do for a living? Actually, hold on for a second. Let me ask a different question. Is there anyone who *wants* to die? If I need to shoot someone else, why not shoot someone who wants to die. Anyone?"

A woman raised her hand.

"Go ahead. Tell me your name and why you want to die."

"My name is Carol Brown. I'm 66 and have terminal cancer. I am only expected to live another month or so. I don't want to die. I don't want to be shot. But if I can save someone else from being killed, and I'm going to die anyway, I would consider doing that."

"Carol, that's very brave and generous of you. 'Selfless' describes it even better. You are willing to give your life to save another. That is very moving. Let me see a show of hands. Who else is willing to give their life to save another?"

"I see a few hands, mostly older folks. Thank you. You can put your hands down. The rest of you are not so generous. So Carol, have you said your goodbyes?"

"Pretty much. Everyone knows I could go at any time."

"All right, we'll get back to you, Carol. Back to you with the plaid shirt: name, age and occupation."

"My name is Frank Johnson. I'm forty-four and I'm a commercial pilot."

"Frank, have you ever been on a hijacked plane?"

"No. This is my first."

"Okay Frank, good answer. Straight and direct. So Frank, why do you think I have hijacked this plane?"

"Well, I don't know for sure but my guess is payback of some kind."

"Payback is a good answer. I was born and raised in Iraq. I went to college in New York to be a computer designer. I'm from a big family that goes back many generations. Lots of aunts and uncles and nieces and nephews, thirty-five people in my family." Amir paused.

"Do you know how many are alive today after President Bush started a war to destroy our weapons of mass destruction?

"I want you to imagine that you have a big family you love and who love you. I want you to see them, eighteen adults of all ages from twenty-five to ninety-five, and seventeen children of all ages from three months to sixteen years old. Can you imagine having all those people in your family? Can you imagine having your favorites, people you have a special bond with, people you love more than anything else in the world?" Amir paused again and methodically looked into the eyes of every person on the plane, one by one. Finally, he said, "They were all murdered by your bombs and your soldiers. They're all dead." Amir was silent to let it sink in, but he continued to look at the faces of the passengers with his shiny cold eyes. Most were looking down. A few made eye contact.

"Do you know how many died from the war in Iraq since 2003?" No one had an answer nor were they willing to risk guessing. "Let me tell you, because most of you have no idea. A hundred thousand Iraqi soldiers died, 300,000 were wounded. In addition to the 100,000 Iraqi soldiers who died, over 150,000 civilians died from violence directly caused by the war. So that's over 250,000 dead and 300,000 wounded." Amir paused again as he made contact with every face in the cabin.

"Three hundred thousand wounded. It is bad enough to die. It's worse to be wounded. Do you know what it's like to be wounded? How many of you have been in the hospital for more than two weeks? Raise your hands."

A few raised their hands.

"You have no idea what it's like to be wounded from war. Most of the people who are wounded will be in and out of hospitals for the rest of their lives. You may need ten to twenty surgeries to try to fix what's wrong with you, and it will never totally heal or be right again. You will be on drugs for a lifetime. You will forever be in some kind of pain as a constant reminder of your war trauma. You will have difficulty sleeping. You will have nightmares. You will have trouble getting a decent job because some part of you will never function normally. You will have money problems. You will drink and do drugs to cope with the pain and frustration of your life. Many commit suicide because they finally decide their life isn't worth the effort. For most people, being wounded is a slow death that eats away at you for as long as you live.

"Do you know how many American soldiers died in Iraq? Only 4,491. So here is an important question. Was it really necessary to kill 250,000 Iraqi people and wound 300,000 more? Do you think that all Iraqis are evil? You know they're not, if you stop and think about it. People are basically the same all over the world. Yes, of course, there are some despicable monsters, but that is a small group, really. Those who died or were wounded were people just like you who were doing their best to live their lives. And what was the cause of this war? Weapons of mass destruction that were never found. The experts today say there was never any substantial proof that they *ever* existed. It was just a clever rumor Saddam made up to scare his enemies.

"So Frank, how do you think the Iraqi people feel about the United States? George Bush and Dick Cheney said the Iraqi people would see the Americans as liberators. Do you think that is how they feel?"

"Probably not," said Frank.

"Can you see how it's possible that the Iraqi people might look at the Americans as terrorists after they killed or wounded 500,000 of their brothers and sisters, all in the name of giving the Iraqis their freedom from a detestable dictator? Can you imagine that the Iraqis are people just like you who can't understand why someone from across the ocean in a far-off land would want to come and kill them over a threat that didn't exist? Do you see how there could be another side to the story?"

"Yes. I can see that."

"So Frank, how would you feel if everyone in your family, everyone you love, was killed by terrorists?"

"It's hard to imagine what that would be like. I would be devastated at first and then I'd be angry. I would want revenge."

"Would you want to kill the murderers who took the lives of your family?"

"Yes. I'm not sure I would have the resources to do that but I would want to kill them."

"Would you be willing to risk your life to get some revenge?"

"Probably."

"I like you, Frank. You have an open mind. You can look at what happened in Iraq and imagine what that would be like if it happened to you. The world would be a better place if every American could take a minute to imagine what it would be like to have your whole family killed in a pointless, needless war.

"So what do you think I should do, Frank? Should I go to a support group to deal with my grief? Or do I become a hero to the folks back home and kill Americans in my spare time?

"Frank, I don't like to kill people. But I feel like it's my moral obligation to honor the death of my family and the hundreds of thousands of my countrymen who were killed or wounded for absolutely no reason. I'm not willing to let Americans go on with their lives like nothing happened. You go to Sunday brunch or to the mall and say, 'Oh, the Iraq War, I remember that. President Bush dressed up in a pilot's outfit on an aircraft carrier with a banner that said *Mission Accomplished*. Our brave fighting men and women won that war!'

"Frank, do you see my dilemma?"

"Yes, I do."

"I am going to take a break for a few minutes, and then we will continue our conversations."

Amir headed for the bathroom at the front of the plane. He walked in but did not close the door. We could hear him relieving himself. I felt something happening behind me. I turned and saw a big, scared middle-aged man moving quickly up the aisle toward the front of the plane, waving for others to follow him like he was going to attack Amir. The guy was moving too fast. No one was following him. A couple of the men thought about getting up but didn't get past sitting forward in their seats. Then he was at my row. I quietly signaled for him to stop. He needed to allow time for some reinforcements, but he ignored me and kept moving toward Amir.

I didn't know what to do. It didn't feel right to me to jump in behind this guy. I wanted to support him. He was risking his life for everyone on the plane, but he was moving too fast, all adrenaline and no common sense. Then the earsplitting blast of Amir's gun consumed the cabin one more time. The back of the attacker's head exploded into a spray of blood and pieces of flesh as he slowly collapsed into a pile on the floor of the cabin.

Then Amir looked at the petrified faces staring back at him. "Brave man. Stupid, but brave. You, what's your name?"

"Luke," I said.

"Move this stupid brave man out of the way. Put him in the window seat of row two."

I immediately got up to move the dead man. There was blood everywhere and now it was all over me. A strong metallic smell added to the horror of it all. He was heavy and sweaty and blood was still oozing out of the back of his head. I managed to lift and push the guy into the window seat. Then I looked at Amir to see if he wanted anything else. He pointed me back to my seat.

This dead guy had the right idea. He was probably someone that Robin had been texting about attacking Amir who decided it was up to him to lead the charge. He had the right idea but no sense of timing. Amir had known someone was moving toward him. He had stepped out of the bathroom at exactly the right instant and shot the life out of his assailant. Amir was going to be hard to surprise. Our only option seemed to be to overpower him and accept the likelihood there would be more casualties in the process. That was still better than having him kill all the people on the plane, which I suspected was his plan.

Amir handed me a bottle of water and a couple of towels to wipe off the blood that was all over me.

"Let me have your attention. We are thirty minutes from landing. There is a bomb on this plane that is designed to disable the landing gear. Bombs are unpredictable. There could be more damage than just the landing gear, but either way we are going to crash land. Some of you could be injured or even die, depending on how good the pilots are. If the plane explodes upon landing, it may be hard to get out before you burn to death.

"In case you're wondering, I am willing to die if I have to. I would prefer to escape and do this again. I plan to open the door of the plane as we are landing and then escape into the night once the plane has come to a stop. "One of my ambitions in life is to make flying a very dangerous form of travel in the United States, and now you and many thousands of our brothers and sisters know why I do this.

"As we attempt to land, I will randomly shoot as many of you as I can from the front of the plane. As you may have noticed, I am an excellent marksman, and I have the most lethal handgun that you Americans make. So use your last minutes wisely. Call your loved ones and say your goodbyes, since most of you probably won't make it. But do it quietly and stay seated and no questions."

Amir was clinical in his delivery. I had no doubt he was serious. I had thirty minutes to make something happen. There was still time to take back the plane. The bomb was a new puzzle piece. My guess was that he would wait until the last minute to disable the landing gear because he wanted to get off the plane. The more unpredictable that landing was, the easier he could escape. It was possible we would overshoot the runway or miss it altogether. But *when* the bomb would explode was such an unknown, it probably wouldn't be useful. We would use the explosion to our advantage if we could but we couldn't make it part of the plan.

Unless Amir was distracted, it was unlikely we could overpower him. He could shoot and kill five people in less than a count of three. The only approach we had was one attacker at a time down the narrow aisle. You would have to give the person in front of you room to run, so we would be easy targets even if we were fast. If there were only some way to get attackers to the front of the plane unnoticed, where they could hide to the left and the right in the bulkhead area, with more reinforcements hiding behind the front seats… That would buy us a second or two. If we could surprise Amir, as he turned to one side to shoot, the guy in front of Amir would go for his gun. The guy on the other side would be behind him and close enough to tackle him if we moved fast enough. Then everyone available would jump on the pile. The key would be to keep him from killing everyone before we had a chance to overwhelm him with muscle and weight.

Then the answer came to me. We would wait until he opened the door to the plane. Our success would depend on being ready to move to the front of the plane the second we heard him fumbling with the door to the outside, which would make a bunch of noise as he opened it. I texted Robin the plan to pass on to the team and said they had to be lightning fast and pin-drop quiet.

Then it occurred to me that he could open the door before he blew the bomb. He could open the door anytime below 10,000 feet without fear of being sucked out of the plane. Plus the bomb was likely toward the back of the plane, so any smoke, flames or debris would not come in the open door by the cockpit. He would have thought of that. So we had to be ready fast. He could open the door at any time now. I could tell we were on our final descent.

I texted Robin to tell the guys to watch for my arm signal. When I gave the signal to charge, they would have to move fast. Our lives depended on it. She texted back, saying everyone was ready. Seven in all. Three chargers and four backups. Scared but ready.

Amir had been sitting in the service area opposite the door. He could easily see down the aisle but also didn't want to be bothered with having eye contact with anyone. Then he got up, did a quick look at the passengers, and walked into the bathroom. He left the door open like before and proceeded with his business. He came out and surveyed the cabin for a few seconds. I had the feeling this was it. I texted Robin to tell the guys to get ready. She confirmed, *Waiting 4 signal. Get em Batman!*

Then Amir turned around and moved toward the big exit door. I could hear him fumbling with the release. I figured I would wait another second to make sure he would not poke his head back in the cabin for one final check. Then I heard another mechanical sound. That was it. I jumped up and gave the charge signal as I headed for the left bulkhead. It was only four rows away, so I was there first.

I waved the other guys to hurry with one arm and put my finger to my lips with the other arm to keep everyone else quiet. Then there were several loud noises as Amir opened the door. You could hear the wind and the jet engines were much louder now. You could smell the fresh air. We had all seven guys toward the front of the plane. The only thing that hadn't worked was we couldn't get anyone in the right bulkhead without Amir seeing them. The closest anyone could get on that side of the plane was behind the second row of seats. That took away a major advantage I was counting on. Damn, we couldn't turn back now. We would have to improvise and hope for the best.

Then I had to get people to stop staring at the front of the plane. Their eyes were so big it would have been an immediate warning to Amir that something was up. I pointed my two fingers at my eyes and then emphatically signaled for them to look down, which they eventually did. We were as ready as we were ever going to be.

I was the tip of the sword, the first guy to have contact with Amir. Being a realist, I knew there was a good chance I would not live through this adventure, but I had to block that thought out of my mind. I could move really fast. I was envisioning being so fast I could move the gun away from me before I got shot. Amir was quick. I had to be quicker. I had to muster all of the energy I could find to move as fast as possible. It was like getting ready to do a karate chop on a cement block. I had to give it 110 percent of all my energy and totally believe I could do it.

We couldn't see Amir. There was way too much noise now to hear anything he did. Then I saw Amir's gun slowly make its way into the cabin right in front of me. I waited for one more split second and then karate chopped his arm so hard I could hear it break. The gun fell to the floor. Then I grabbed Amir's shoulders and knocked his legs out from under him so he would fall to the floor. I knew he could fall on top of me, but I would try to get to the side on the way to the floor and then do my best to hold him down, awaiting reinforcements.

Right on cue, everyone jumped on top of us, and a wrestling match ensued that would have won the praise of the WWF. One of the attackers was a bodybuilder. He hit Amir so hard in the face I thought he killed him. Then there was the hauntingly familiar blast of Amir's gun, the last thing I wanted to hear. I looked to see how that was possible because Amir didn't have his gun.

Then I realized one of the guys had grabbed for the gun and had accidentally pulled the hair trigger. I felt an intense pain in my chest right near my heart. The red spot on my shirt got bigger really fast. I started to feel light-headed and then I couldn't see or move. The wrestling continued for a few more seconds and then I heard the unmistakable sound of duct tape. A lot of duct tape. I couldn't see what they were doing, but I hoped they were being thorough. There was a resounding cheer from the passengers. Amir was in submission. We had done it!

Then I could hear someone say, "Did anyone get shot?"

"I think he said his name was Luke," said one of the men.

"That's Batman," one of the other men said. "He's saved us all!"

"Is he okay?"

"He got shot in the heart."

I felt fingers on my neck checking for a pulse and then a voice reluctantly said, "He's gone."

A couple of the guys put me in a seat next to the dead guy in row 2 to get me out of the way. They thought I was dead! I couldn't speak and I couldn't move. They must be able to see I was still breathing! I must have a pulse. I had to be careful not to panic. I had to calm down. I had to remember my ability to

175

find my center and block out the fear. I could feel warmth and love around my heart. It was a strange, wonderful feeling that was hard to comprehend at the time. The intuitive message I was clearly getting was to relax and wait. My intellect was in total panic. It felt more right to go with the positive feeling and ignore the negative.

The next thing I remember was the distinct bump of the wheels hitting the ground. We had landed on a runway and came to a controlled stop. Amir did not get to blow up the landing gear after all. I could hear people cheering again with delight and relief in their voices. We didn't taxi for long before we stopped and passengers were quickly taken off the plane, probably because the bomb was still a potential threat. I could hear their voices disappearing out the open front door.

Suddenly I felt warm and tender hands on my wrist and then my neck. A woman's voice yelled, "This man is still alive! Get the EMTs up here with a stretcher and equipment *stat*!"

That was sweet music to my ears. I could put to rest any terrifying thoughts of being buried alive that were lingering outside my circle of protection. Now I just had to figure out a way to get my eyes open.

Within seconds I was being attended to by what seemed like a team of medics. One person put an IV in my hand, another was cutting my shirt open, and another was putting a thermometer in my mouth.

"Mr. Lamaire, can you hear me? I'm Dr. Julie. I'm going to be taking care of you this evening. Mr. Lamaire, squeeze my hand if you can hear me. Come on, darlin', you can do it. Squeeze my hand. Let me know someone's home in there."

I channeled all the energy I had and finally managed to move my hand enough so she could feel it.

"Houston, we have a squeeze... Mr. Lamaire, we're going to take good care of you." She turned away from me, but I could still hear her soft voice. "He's amazingly stable. The only injury we can find is the gunshot wound to the chest. We have the bleeding stopped, but it could start again any second. I have no idea why his injury isn't more severe. He was shot close range with a cannon. He can't move or speak yet. Let's carefully get him to the hospital. I'll ride with you."

I could sense she was looking at me again. "Mr. Lamaire, we're going to take you to the hospital so we can take better care of you. It's just down the street. You ready to take a ride with us? If you understand, squeeze my hand... Got the squeeze. Let's roll."

Being able to do simple things like see and speak and move your body is easy to take for granted. I would be forever grateful to have those functions back to normal as soon as possible. Meanwhile, people were talking to me and asking me questions as if they thought I might respond. I was being gently moved around and treated with the utmost vigilance. The ambulance door closed. There were two loud bangs on the door. Then the intensely loud whine of the siren was a bit ominous as the driver floored it like we were in a drag race. That was a moment I will always remember. It should have been cause for concern, but there was a calm presence that kept me from worrying. I was being communicated with in a way that I had never experienced before. A calm voice was clearly speaking to me now but there was no sound. Maybe it was a form of telepathy. The message was clear: *relax, you'll be fine.*

I vaguely remember people asking me questions and not being able to respond for a long time. I wanted to respond, but I just didn't have the strength. Then Dr. Julie asked me if I had a girlfriend... I was instantly able to open my eyes and saw blinding bright lights and several people in masks and hoods standing over me doing something to my chest. Then I somehow managed to say, "Yes, I do."

"Mr. Lamaire, welcome back! Nice to have you with us again. And I'm sure your girlfriend is going to be glad to hear that you've joined the party. What's your girlfriend's name?"

"Sophia."

"Such a pretty name. You're a lucky guy, Mr. Lamaire, in more ways than you know."

"Call me Luke."

"Okay, Luke, that's much easier. Luke, we need to have you lie very still for a while longer. We took a bullet out of your chest that was very close to your heart. Do you remember being shot?"

"I do. It hurt."

"Luke, would you believe that everyone I know who's been shot has said that very same thing? It hurts like hell. Are you feeling any pain right now?"

"No."

"Do you feel anything in the area around your chest?"

"No."

"That's what we want to hear. We numbed you up pretty good so we could take out the bullet. You aren't going to feel much of anything for a while but that's normal. Can you make a fist with your right hand for me? That's good. How about the other hand? Good. Can you wiggle your toes? Very good. You're gonna be fine, Luke. Just give us a little more time to finish up and you'll be good as new."

"I wasn't able to move or speak," I said.

"I know what that's like. And we want to hear more about that, but let's do that later, okay? Right now, I just want you to relax and think good thoughts while we finish getting you ready for action... I heard that Sophia is on her way here right now on a private jet. Either *she* is a very important person or *you* are a very important person. Who's more important, you or her?"

"*She* is."

"I know she'll be glad to hear you feel that way. I need more suction over here. Pardon me, Luke. We're just making sure everything looks good before we close you up. When was the last time you saw Sophia?"

"It seems like a long time. A couple days?"

"Sounds like you think Sophia is pretty special."

"She is."

"I look forward to meeting her. Looks good, Dr. Joe. Close him up. Luke, are you comfortable? Do you feel any pain?"

"No."

"Luke, I am done here and needed elsewhere. It's been a busy night. If you need anything, just tell Dr. Joe and he'll take care of you. We good?"

I slowly managed to reach my hand out to Dr. Julie. She pulled off her glove and held my hand.

"Thanks, Doc, for taking care of me."

"You're very welcome. You've been a star patient. We like success stories around here and you're gonna be one of them."

"Thanks again, Doc."

"I'll be back to check on you. It's late so it won't be until tomorrow. By the way, you're a major sensation on the news. They're calling you…and let me see if I can get this right. You're the man who saved the Los Angeles-to-New York Flight 224 from the terrorist-killer-bomber who was shot by the terrorist, left for dead and then later discovered to be alive, code name Batman. Does any of that sound vaguely familiar?" She smiled and waited for it to sink in.

"Wow, I'd kind of forgotten about all that."

"I suspected as much. Just to bring you up-to-date, we are fighting to keep reporters out of here. Your girlfriend put two very large armed bodyguards outside your door who go by the names of Nemo and Frédo. Nice guys, actually.

"The only people who have permission to see you or talk to you are immediate family members. We will add Sophia to the list and give Nemo and Frédo limited access so they can do their job. Sophia will be here in a few hours, so you need to get some rest. You're going to feel groggy and sleepy for a few days. You basically had the equivalent of major heart surgery. Everything was textbook, so we expect a full recovery, but you're going to need to take things slow and easy to give your body time to heal. Will you do that for me?"

"I'll do it, Doc. Thanks for handling the details. I owe ya."

"Again, you're welcome. And there are about a hundred people who say they probably wouldn't be alive if it weren't for your courage. So you're already a special guy in our book, and it's probably more fitting to say that we are the ones that owe *you*."

"Thanks, Doc."

17. Recovery...

When I woke up, there she was, the love of my life. She looked like she'd been crying, but that just added to her beauty and presence.

"Hey you, what a nice surprise," I said quietly.

"Oh, thank God, you're awake." She hurried over to me from the makeshift desk she had created to work on her computer. She put her hands on my face, looked at me with tears running down her cheeks, and gave me a long kiss.

"I am so glad you're okay." She was holding herself back from crying.

"It's obviously not time for me to go yet. We have too many things to do together."

In that moment, she let it all go and just sobbed. I held her hand and opened myself up to her to feel whatever I could. There was a torrent of emotion behind her usual loving manner, and she wasn't holding anything back. I had never seen anyone cry with that much intensity. After a few rounds, she began to talk as best she could.

"Rachel called me to tell me you had been shot and you were dead. I couldn't do anything but sit there and keep saying, 'This isn't happening, this isn't possible.' Then thirty minutes later, Rachel calls me again and tells me you're alive. That felt more right to me but I was afraid. Then a few minutes later, Dr. Julie tells me you *should* be dead but you're not and they're rushing you to the hospital for emergency surgery. I was afraid to find out what had really happened to you.

"I had to hold it together for the plane ride. Then when I finally got here, the staff that knew who I was had gone home. They said no one but immediate family. I finally said, 'I'm his wife!' and they let me right in. Then once I saw you…I knew you were okay."

"That's the truth. I'm going to be okay. They expect a full recovery."

"I knew you meant a lot to me. But I had no idea how much until someone told me you were dead. That was the most horrible, depressing thing I've ever felt."

"Sorry to be so over-the-top. I know how you hate it when I'm too dramatic." That got a little smile.

"I feel better," she said. I could hear a sigh of relief. Then she took a few more seconds to catch her breath and blow her nose. "I haven't had a good cry in a long time. I haven't allowed myself to cry about anything until this happened."

"Glad I could help."

"You're just out of emergency surgery, and you're making jokes!"

"That's why you love me."

"You're right, I do love you." I got another sustained kiss. Then she pulled a chair up close to the side of the bed. "I'm starting to feel seminormal even though part of me feels like I've been run over by a large truck. We have more to talk about."

"Something important?"

"Let's find out." She was excited about something. "When I talked to Dr. Julie on my way over here, she said you should be dead. She said the bullet didn't go in that far and that was good because it was headed for your heart. It just made you bleed a lot. She said the other victims had been shot at a much greater distance and had massive exit wounds. She said there is no logical reason the bullet didn't go right through you and make a bigger mess on the way out, like all the others. I can think of only one explanation."

"And that would be?"

"You were protected."

"What do you mean?"

"Did anything seem different to you?"

"Do you mean was I surprised at my ability to remain calm when someone put their fingers to my neck to see if I was alive and then said 'He's gone,' and pushed me off to the side with the other dead bodies? Or was I surprised at the voice that was talking to me without making any sound telling me to relax and that everything would be fine?"

"You heard a voice that didn't make any sound. How did you feel when you heard the voice?"

"Strangely calm, peaceful. I believed what I was hearing. I believed that everything would be okay and that I could just relax."

"You did it! You reached lightspace." There were tears in her eyes again, but this was different. "One of the first things you feel is great protection. You were protected because you reached lightspace. The voices that don't make any sound are your new connection with the Source."

"It occurred to me that lightspace might be a factor," I said with a smile.

"Oh, my, God, you reached lightspace, and you did it on your own. I'm so proud of you. And just in time. We could have lost you. I want more details, but I can tell I'd better wait until you have more energy and you're not so high on painkillers."

"Is that what's making me feel like I'm floating? I thought it was your kisses."

"I'm still being amazed. Not that I had any doubt you would do it. I didn't think you would do it this fast. And that's why you're alive. Unbelievable."

"I think it's time for a short nap."

"Before you doze off…just a couple of quick items?"

"Okay," I said reluctantly.

"You have gotten calls from your mom, your sister and a few hundred of your closest friends. What do you want me to do with them?"

"Call my mother and my sister and tell them I'm okay and not awake much yet. The rest will have to wait."

"You realize that you're a major celebrity all over the world for what you did on that plane?"

"I haven't had much time to think about that. It feels more like a dream. By the way, who's Rachel?" I asked.

"The flight attendant that you were working with on the plane."

"Oh, that's Robin. We didn't use our real names."

"How did you come up with *Robin*?"

"Batman's sidekick."

"Of course. How did I miss that?" she said, rolling her eyes.

"And how did you get to New York so fast?"

"Jean Claude is here in New York. He was watching on TV and the Internet like we all were. He has a friend who keeps his jet in Santa Monica. One phone call from Jean Claude and we were wheels up in twenty minutes, and I was here in record time."

"That's awesome."

"It felt like they loved being able to do Jean Claude a favor. And those guys were so nice to me even though I was a total mess."

"I'm sure they could see what you were going through."

"Oh, and Lon Prince said *he* will fly to Los Angeles to meet *you* whenever you're ready. He said to tell you nice job stopping the bad guy. He was glued to the TV. And he wished you a speedy recovery."

"That's good news. I have a feeling Lon will be important to us."

Sophia stayed a couple of days and worked while I was sleeping, which was often. It was a special time for us even though the circumstances weren't ideal. Our bond and our connection to each other had gone way beyond whatever it had been before. Then we agreed it was important to get her back to L.A. to direct the Project. There was just too much at stake. That she had made the trip and spent two days with me even though I was fuzzy from the drugs had a major impact on my recovery. Looking at her every time I woke up locked in the biggest incentive I'd ever had to get well and come back stronger than ever. Often people get depressed when they are sick or injured. I felt like the luckiest guy in the world who had been given a second chance and a mandate to make some big things happen that were in my grasp.

They released me from the hospital after a week. I could have gone home sooner, but they wanted to make sure I was ready to fly, plus the hospital loved the publicity. They couldn't find room for all the flowers and cards and mail—not to mention the amount of email—that came every day. I had steady calls coming in from people I knew and tons more from people I had never met. Everyone meant well, but it was actually exhausting to have the same conversations over and over. I could screen the calls to some degree with caller ID, but many of the numbers were unidentifiable so I had to listen to endless voicemails.

Jean Claude was still in New York and offered to fly me back to Santa Monica on *his* jet. That sounded good to me. Getting on a commercial flight was not my first preference, if I had a choice. Even if the odds were more likely that I would be struck by lightning before I would end up on another hijacked plane, being shot had surfaced emotions both good and bad. I appreciated being alive more than ever before. Now every second counted for something, and I suspected that

185

would always be the case. Lightspace was about living in the present moment, so all of that was a positive.

On the other side, being shot was extremely painful and the rehab was like climbing a mountain every day. I hated being on any kind of drugs but the pain was intense. Every once in a while I would get angry at the sap who had shot me. Everything would have worked so well if he had just not grabbed at Amir's gun. But then I would remember all the extraordinary things that happened to me because I got shot.

Angela, the staff counselor, told me I was lucky because I was not shot in anger. She had worked with gunshot victims who took a long time to get back to normal because someone had *tried* to kill them. She said some people never give up that anger, which keeps them from ever having any peace of mind.

The weeks went by. I kept doing physical therapy to get my strength back. The healing process was gaining some momentum. I could work for a few hours before I needed a nap. I mostly made phone calls and did meetings in the office. I tried to spend as much time at the ASC office as I could because I got so much energy being around all the great people. Sophia and I tried to spend more time together. She was so busy most of the time it was still difficult.

Then last night, I got a call from Sophia around 7 p.m. I was out cold taking my evening nap. She asked me if I wanted to come over to her place. She had gotten me a present that had arrived in the mail and wanted to give it to me. Her dinner meeting had cancelled and she wanted to hang out. Music to my tired ears. She sent Diego to pick me up. I was getting lots of limo rides during my recovery, which I loved.

When I got to her place, the door was ajar. I knocked and was invited in from the next room. She told me to sit down on the couch and she would be right out with my surprise.

A couple more minutes went by. I was waiting patiently with growing curiosity to see what she had cooked up. Then she gracefully walked out into the middle of the room like a model on a runway. She stopped a couple of feet in front of me to pose and then turned around and posed again like a professional model. I was impressed. She had on a black cutoff T-shirt that barely covered her naked breasts that I so enjoyed keeping track of—off duty, of course. In very fancy white sequined lettering the T-shirt said, *I did it upside-down with Batman!*

I laughed. "I'm not sure what that means exactly."

"I'm not either," she said. "But it sounded right, and I figured Batman and I would come up with something creative."

"That's a job description I can get behind."

I got a suggestive glance. Then she turned away from me, put her hands on her hips, and said, "Do you like my socks?" She had tall, white, over-the-calf basketball socks with words printed vertically on the back. On her left sock at the top were big letters that spelled *BAT*. On the top of the right sock was the word *MAN*.

"I love the cheerleader look," I said.

"Funny you should say that. I was thinking I might inspire Batman with a routine I used to do as a high school cheerleader."

"You must really like Batman."

"I *love* Batman."

"Buying that T-shirt was a little presumptuous before the fact…"

"I was hoping Batman would see this T-shirt and want to make my dream come true."

"Batman aims to please."

"Can I get you something cool to drink, my caped wonder? You look a little flushed."

"I'd love a glass of Pinot. Then get back over here. I can't get enough of this great new look. I've seen fashion shows before but I can't remember a single outfit. I can confidently say that what you've modeled for me tonight I will never forget!"

I should mention that the cutoff T-shirt and the tall basketball socks were *all* Sophia was wearing. Even though I was still not physically 100 percent, we managed to make our first time an evening we will fondly remember. As Sophia so aptly put it, my recovery was a reason to take our time and really enjoy each other. God, what a woman!

18. The Show...

Our broadcasts were going out to thousands of people all over the world, so Sophia had a TV studio built in the ASC headquarters. Candy had the production and technical skills, so she became the TV producer for the LightSpace Television Network. It was all very exciting. Sophia was such a popular speaker and interviewer, she was being asked to be on many other shows as well.

"Luke, let's see how you look," said Candy. "You're nice and tan so you don't need makeup. I like the open-shirt-and sport-coat look on you." She put her pen in her mouth and her clipboard under her arm so she could press the lapels on my coat and brush some lint from my shoulder. Then I got a smile and a wink. "You look good."

"Thank you, Candy. Where do you want me?"

She whispered in my ear, "You know where I want you, lover." She gave me a second to get her naughty reference and then she smiled. "Stand right here. You're on in three minutes."

I would have to reconsider my covert mergers with Candy in light of new developments with Sophia. I enjoyed my naked time with Candy, but I was in love with Sophia. I hated to limit my lovemaking partners, but keeping peace in the henhouse felt like a bigger priority. Maybe when everyone reached lightspace, all that pesky possessiveness will be more relaxed. That's a good question for Sophia. Write that down.

"Okay, handsome, I just got the signal," said Candy. "Quietly and slowly walk in and sit down next to Sophia. Don't say anything until she speaks to you. Off you go. Break a leg!"

I found my seat while Sophia was finishing with a person calling in from London.

"That's all the time we have for our Q&A today," said Sophia. "Thank you, everyone, for participating. We had some great questions, and hopefully you feel like you got some good answers from our panel. I thought they were excellent. And thank you to our panel, as always. We appreciate your time and commitment to our cause.

"My next guest needs no introduction. He is a VIP with the LightSpace Project, but many more know Luke Lamaire as the guy who saved over a hundred people from certain disaster on Flight 224 from L.A. to New York this past month. Luke orchestrated the overpowering of a hijacker with five of the passengers. Several of the passengers had been shot and killed before they were able to neutralize their captor. And Luke himself was shot and left for dead after a fierce battle in the cabin of the plane. Obviously, Luke is alive and we are thrilled to have him here with us today. Welcome, Luke."

"Thank you, Sophia. Needless to say, I'm glad to be here."

"Luke, you've told your story a million times by now, so we're not going to ask you to go over all those details today. What we *do* want to hear about is how lightspace was a factor in your ability to overcome the hijacker and be alive to talk about it."

"Absolutely one of my favorite things to talk about. Let's start with basics. Lightspace is the ability to live in the present moment guided by the smartest part of your brain, your intuitive instincts. You have to learn to get the intellectual misperceptions we all have out of the way. This helps you lessen your concern over the past and your fear of the future so you can focus on listening for the path you are given by your intuition.

"One of the results of learning to think this way is an increased ability to be calm in the face of danger. When the plane was hijacked, I had to be able to work the problem without letting my emotions get in the way. And even when you think you have the best plan in place, things can go wrong, which they did. You have to be ready to improvise in a split second and not look back."

"Sounds intense. So were you scared you were going to get shot?" asked Sophia.

"I knew I was going to be the first guy to attack the hijacker. We had already seen how fast and accurate he was with his gun when he shot the first three passengers. I knew there was a good chance I was not going to make it."

"Were you scared or were you calm?" asked Sophia.

"I was surprisingly calm. I was able to put my fears aside and focus on what I had to do."

"Amazing, Luke. What else can you tell us about the LightSpace Training that helped you?"

"Sure. There are several things you have to be extremely good at to get to lightspace. You have to be able to hold a positive vision of the future, no matter what the circumstances. You have to trust your intuitive instincts as if your life depended on it. If you get too analytical, you lose your edge and you're toast. Essentially, you have to commit to what feels intuitively right and give it everything you've got. That's being in the zone of lightspace."

"Are you in that zone now?"

"You bet. Certainly some situations are more demanding than others, but you never stop using the LightSpace Formula as I just described it. It becomes a way of life."

"People often ask me, '*Do you have to believe in God to get to lightspace?* '"

"Lightspace doesn't work without free will. So the answer is not necessarily a yes or a no. You want to choose to do what feels right and stay away from what doesn't feel right to the best of your ability. For most people, as you move away from being a separated ego toward being an intuitive spirit, you discover a relationship with your spirit that you never had before. You actually interact with that spirit. People like to give a name to whoever or whatever is on the other end of that new relationship. Some call it their *Higher Self.* Some call it their *God Self.* You get to call it whatever you want. It's very personal."

"Here's the question I get asked the most, *'How do you know when you have reached lightspace?'*"

"It's a little different for everyone, of course. But there are similarities. There's a greatly increased sense of protection from negativity of all kinds. The only reason I'm here today is because of the protection of lightspace. I was shot in the heart with a large-caliber handgun at close range. The bullet caused a lot of bleeding but it didn't do any permanent damage. Another aspect is that you feel an obligation to act on your intuitive promptings like you've never felt before. Life becomes much simpler in many ways. You do what feels intuitively right whether you like it or not. It's a discipline and the results speak for themselves."

"Luke, we have twenty seconds for one final question. *Did you feel a calling to reach lightspace?*"

"That's a tougher question. I've always felt a calling, but for a long time it was to the wrong things. It wasn't until I joined the LightSpace Project that I discovered my *real* calling."

"And we are so glad you did. Luke, thank you for your time today. I know you are incredibly busy. We appreciate you taking a few minutes to talk with us."

"You're very welcome."

"That's our show for today, people. I want to close with a quote from a man you will all recognize: *The intuitive mind is*

*a sacred gift, the intellectual mind is a faithful servant. We
have created a society that honors the servant and has
forgotten the gift.* Albert Einstein.

"Thanks for joining us. We will do this again soon. Until
then, trust and act on what feels intuitively right. Miracles will
happen! This is Sophia Forlani for the LightSpace Television
Network saying goodbye for now."

"And we are off the air," announced Candy.

There was an immediate burst of noise and activity. Sophia
looked at me. "Nice job, champ."

"Back to ya," I said. "Always a pleasure to be interviewed
by the First Lady of LightSpace."

"Don't call me that. It makes me sound old and stodgy. Plus
I've noticed that the nicknames you give people tend to stick,
so let's come up with something a little more flattering. Will
you do that for me?"

"Of course, Your Majesty."

"That's worse!" I got a playful shove from my disapproving
partner.

"What's next?" I said.

"Jean Claude is making a surprise visit and taking us all out
for lunch. We have a private room at the Chart House. He said
he has an important announcement to make. Candy made a
reservation for you. I assumed you could make it. We just
found out."

"Count me in. Sounds like it's good news," I said.

The Chart House was just south of the ASC office in
Marina del Rey. The upper-end restaurant chain was known
for its spectacular views, and this place was no exception.
Fancy food and a breathtaking view of the water were my
favorite combination for a business meeting and, hopefully, a
celebration.

Everyone from the ASC office, a couple of guests, some
spouses and a few friends who were available on short notice
were in attendance enjoying lavish hors d'oeuvres. Jean

Claude was en route from the Santa Monica Airport, where he had just landed his jet. The atmosphere was electric.

Sophia made the announcement to about thirty of us. "If everyone would find a place at the table. Jean Claude has arrived and is on a tight schedule. He wants to say a few words to the group before we have lunch. So please be seated."

As people were getting settled, Jean Claude blew into the room with his cell phone to his ear and his hand on the receiver while he gave instructions to his personal assistant. His two bodyguards found their strategic spots. Jean Claude found his place at the head of the table. We said quick hellos and then he moved to the podium to address the group.

"Bonjour, mes amis."

The crowd responded, *"Bonjour,* Jean Claude."

"It is my great pleasure to be here with you and see all your happy faces. I appreciate everyone gathered here today. This luncheon is to celebrate a job well done and to announce our next challenge."

Jean Claude turned away from the microphone to tell Sophia to make sure everyone had a glass of champagne.

"We have heard from the LightSpace Board of Directors. That's not actually their name, but that's what we like to call them." There were smiles and quiet laughter. "They like what we have done in our first month of operation, which is cause for celebration.

"I know you are all working as hard as you can. Obviously, for us who know the truth, the price of failure this time is unthinkable. So we face our great challenge with a resolute belief that we can succeed, along with an unshakeable vow to do our intuitive best. Guided by this light, we cannot fail. Plus, I am convinced they picked the right people for this challenge to save our world. How do *you* feel about that?"

The room broke into resounding applause and cheers.

"The vision is to develop a worldwide organization of people who are devoted to being intuitive spirits. If everyone in the world only did what felt intuitively right, the world would instantly become a place beyond our wildest dreams. Achieving lightspace is the process of transcending the selfish, fearful ego to become the loving, creative, intuitive spirit that we really are. If enough of us can overcome the resistance of our petty egos, God has promised us the Kingdom.

"So the good news is that we are off to an impressive start. The more challenging news is that we were just informed that we have ninety days to get 10 percent of the world population to lightspace or it's all over."

The room became totally still with numerous open mouths of disbelief.

"In France, we say *Santè*, which means *to your health and long life*. In light of these circumstances, this is a profound sentiment. So raise your glasses. A toast to you, to all of us as a team, and to your unconditional commitment to achieving our goal. *Santè!*"

About the Author

Sidney C. Walker

Sid Walker is a pioneer, an innovator, and a seeker of empowering solutions to the challenges we face in sales and spiritual evolution.

By age twenty-eight, Sid had several Fortune 500 clients as an executive outplacement coach. Hearing a call to expand his coaching skills, Sid found *New York Times* best-selling author Dr. Cherie Carter Scott, who is considered the mother of coaching. Sid was certified as a coach by her training company, Motivation Management Service (theMMS.com), in 1982.

In 1988, Sid wrote his first book, *Trusting YourSelf* (updated to **Trust Your Gut** in 2004). He then focused exclusively on the financial services industry as a coach. To date, Sid has coached more than 2,000 advisors. He is the founder of

SellingWithoutWrestling.com, an extensive training site for advisors who are advocates of the low-key or no sales pressure approach. A large percentage of Sid's coaching clients have become sales production leaders in their industry.

Sid has written a collection of nonfiction softcover books, ebooks and hundreds of articles. His best-selling book is ***How to Double Your Sales by Asking a Few More Questions***.

The passion that now drives Sid is to help people move away from the restrictions of the selfish ego and develop a stronger relationship with their intuitive spirit. After rising to the leadership level of many contemporary training programs and thousands of hours as a personal coach to many talented and gifted people, Sid found the message he wants to share in *The LightSpace Ultimatum*.

Sid currently has an individual coaching practice and does periodic tele-webinars and limited speaking engagements. **For current contact information**, go to SidWalker.com.

LightSpace.us

If you would like to be first to hear about new book releases, sign up for my ***New Release Mailing List*** at:

www.LightSpace.us

Resources

Some of my favorite resources related to achieving lightspace:

Paramahansa Yogananda (Yogananda-SRF.org). My favorite spiritual author and meditation resource, brilliantly clear and understandable. Many practical books, booklets, and audio on how to live life to its fullest. Self-Realization Fellowship is the name of the organization in the US.

Landmark Education (LandmarkEducation.com). Group training on how to be more effective in fulfilling what's important to you by having more power, freedom and full self-expression. There is a free presentation by a master trainer every month in major cities. They don't advertise—you have to be invited. You are now officially invited to check out this resource. Seriously consider doing the initial training, called The Forum. It is a weekend everyone should experience. The basic training is now being taught in nine languages in over 30 countries.

Motivation Management Service (theMMS.com). *New York Times* best-selling author Dr. Cherie Carter Scott and her sister Lynn Stewart are my intuitive coaching mentors. They have been leaders in the coaching field since 1975 and are experts on how to get past negativity, blocked feelings, and the barriers to finding your authentic self.

Books by Timothy Gallway: *The Inner Game of Tennis*, *The Inner Game of Golf* and *Inner Skiing*. Sports coach and business consultant with a profound and practical understanding of the power of intuition.

Books by Eric Butterworth: *In the Flow of Life* and *Spiritual Economics*. Past Unity minister and master of "staying in the flow," backing it all up with scripture.

Financial Success – Harnessing the Power of Creative Thought by Wallace Wattles. Written in 1910, a book with a message important enough to reread every couple of years.

You Can't Afford the Luxury of a Negative Thought – A Book for People with Any Life-Threatening Illness Including Life by Peter McWilliams. A comprehensive encyclopedia on positive thinking endorsed by both Oprah Winfrey and Larry King.

The War of Art – Break Through the Blocks and Win Your Inner Creative Battles by Steven Pressfield. By the author of *The Legend of Bagger Vance*, subsequently produced as a feature film by Robert Redford. Invaluable book on how to get past whatever is keeping you from doing something creative or anything else you want to do.

The Gift of Change – Spiritual Guidance for a Radically New Life by Marianne Williamson. A contemporary, clear voice on how to live a spiritually guided life. From her book description: "The only real failure is the failure to grow from what we go through by reorienting ourselves using an eternal compass of spiritual principles."

A Guide to the I Ching by Carol K. Anthony. The most easy-to-read English interpretation of the 5,000-year-old Chinese book of philosophy, which is big on putting more trust in the path of the Creative (God), less focus on the ego/intellect.

How to Argue and Win Every Time by Gerry Spence. The cowboy defense attorney who won many big cases with a win/win approach offers a perceptive perspective on the importance of making an argument for what you value. A regular guest commentator on NBC News for years.

Other Books by
Sidney C. Walker
(Nonfiction)

TRUST YOUR GUT – How to Overcome the Obstacles to Greater Success and Self-fulfillment.

HOW TO DOUBLE YOUR SALES BY ASKING A FEW MORE QUESTIONS – Making More Sales by Helping People Get What THEY Really Want.

THE PROSPECTING MENTALITY – How to Overcome Call Reluctance, Procrastination, and Sleepless Nights.

HOW TO GET MORE COMFORTABLE ASKING FOR REFERRALS

Write a Review...
It's easy and it's good karma!

With thousands of books being published *every day*, getting a positive review is a bigger deal to authors than you might think. In the online world, the success of a book is largely determined by the number of positive reviews.

If you like something about a book, write a review. A couple of sentences are all you need along with a summary title line. Of course, you can write more.

Answer any of the following questions and you've got a review...

What did you like about the book?
What did you find valuable about the book?
What positive experience did you get from reading the book?
What did you relate to the most?
What moved you?
What made you feel something important?
What insight(s) did you get from reading the book?
Did the book change how you will approach life in any way?
Was there anything different about this book that you liked?
Does this book remind you of any other book(s) you have read?

The authors of the world collectively thank you for your thoughtfulness and generosity!

41202228R00134

Made in the USA
Charleston, SC
22 April 2015